# BLIND FAITH

BLIND FAITH SERIES, BOOK ONE

N.R. WALKER

# COPYRIGHT

Cover Artist: Sara York
Blind Faith © 2013 N.R. Walker
Second edition: February 2013
Published by N.R. Walker

## All Rights Reserved:

This literary work may not be reproduced or transmitted in any form or by any means, including electronic or photographic reproduction, in whole or in part, without express written permission except in the case of brief quotations embodied in critical articles and reviews.
This is a work of fiction and any resemblance to persons, living or dead, or business establishments, events or locales is coincidental.
The Licensed Art Material is being used for illustrative purposes only.

## Warning

This book contains material that maybe offensive to some and is intended for a mature, adult audience. It contains graphic language, explicit sexual content and adult situations.

## Trademarks Acknowledgement

The author acknowledges the trademarked status and trademark owners of the following wordmarks mentioned in this work of fiction:

*Ford Taurus:* Ford Motor Company

*Jeep:* Chrysler Group LLC.

*Scrabble:* Hasbro Inc.

*Monopoly:* Hasbro Inc.

*Jell-O:* Kraft Foods Group

*iPhone:* Apple Inc.

*Ralph Lauren*: PRL US Holdings Inc.

*Armani:* Giorgio Armani S.p.A.

## DEDICATION

*For Jules...*

# 1

I always thought a person's car was reflective of its owner, and as I opened the passenger door of the late '80s Ford Taurus and got in, I smiled to myself. Like its owner, Dr Fields, it was gray in color and in impeccable condition. Not a scratch, not a dent, not a thing out of place. Polished, tidy, and clean. Family oriented, safety first. Just like its owner.

And although it still ran well, although it was still reliable, it was getting on in miles, years. Just like its owner.

Was my car reflective of me? As much as I wished otherwise—yeah, it was. A sturdy Jeep 4x4, a few dents and scratches. Not too old, and certainly not showroom-pretty by any means. More rugged, well-worn, sometimes fun, always practical. That's me. Practical for my work as a vet, practical for me on days off to harness my dog in the backseat and head out of town. Nothing about my car strictly screamed "gay man" but nothing about me did either.

Unless you counted the small star decal on the rear bumper.

My best friend Mark had stuck it there before I'd left Hartford, Connecticut to start my new job in Boston. He'd known I'd bury myself in my work like I always did, limiting my chances of meeting anyone new. He had told me by having a star stuck on my rear bumper, it might increase the chances of some guy seeing the one tattooed on my hip. He'd said the star was more discreet than the "I'm gay. Wanna fuck?" decal he was going to put on my car. He thought it was hilarious. Mark always thought he was hilarious.

"What's got you smiling?" Dr Fields asked.

I looked at the older man behind the steering wheel. "Oh, nothing," I said dismissively. But I looked at him and smiled.

He smiled back at me. Then the older man asked, "How are you settling in? You enjoying it here?"

"Yes," I answered him honestly. "Very much. I mean, it's only been a week, but I love what I've seen so far." And I did. My new job at East Weymouth Animal Hospital was quite the step up for me.

He smiled again, seemingly pleased with his decision to hire me.

He concentrated on driving for a moment, then he asked, "Did you do house calls in Hartford?"

I laughed. "Uh, no. I thought house calls were something doctors and vets did in small country towns for large animals." *Or in television shows*, I thought errantly, but kept that to myself.

This time it was Dr Fields who laughed. "Well, there's not many house calls left on my books these days. Just the families who've been coming to see me for years."

And that's where we were on our way to now. The animal hospital was in a nice part of town, and all house calls were close by. Our first visit was to a Mrs Yeo and her seventeen year old cat, Mr Whiskers. When we got there, I wasn't surprised Mrs Yeo preferred house calls. She must have been

*Blind Faith*

near a hundred years old, all of four feet tall, with gray, wiry hair and skin like wrinkled paper.

"Don't let her appearance fool you," Dr Fields had warned me in the car. "She's as sharp as a tack."

So she was, but poor old Mr Whiskers wasn't doing so well. He was slow and not too responsive as Dr Fields gently checked him over. He gave Mr Whiskers some more arthritis medication, but even Mrs Yeo had given a sad nod, acknowledging she knew the poor tabby's days were numbered.

Against our insistence, Mrs Yeo had walked us out. Dr Fields had given her a reassuring pat on the arm, telling her if she needed anything to give him a call. As we got back into his car, Dr Fields sighed. "I don't think poor Mr Whiskers will see the end of summer," he said sadly. "Not sure how Mrs Yeo will cope without him. She got that cat for company after her husband died…" The older man's words trailed away. He didn't need to say any more. I understood.

It was easy to tell the older man loved his job. I'd only worked with him a week, but he knew every patient and owner by name, and he took his time with each of them. He knew their personal histories. He had an old-school work ethic, and I wondered how his pending retirement would fare on him.

I assumed he'd miss it as much as the hospital would miss him, and from my first week on the job, one thing was very clear—I had very big shoes to fill.

We drove in silence for a short while, and I watched the slow passing of houses through the passenger side window. The animal hospital was in Weymouth, South Boston, which was a nice neighborhood already, but the houses we were driving past were getting even nicer, the gardens and lawns well-tended.

Wanting to keep conversation going between us, I prompted the old man, "Next stop is the Brannigans."

Dr Fields nodded. "Isaac Brannigan..." he said quietly with a shake of his head. "Sad story, but not really mine to tell. Hannah will be there. She's his official caregiver," he said rather cryptically.

I wondered what he meant by that when we pulled into a circular drive. The large, single story house sat proudly in the midst of manicured gardens. It spoke money.

Dr Fields pulled up at the front door, but before he got out of the car, he said, "Isaac's having some adjustment issues with his new dog, Brady. He's a little..." he searched for the right word, "...*insistent*, but I guess he's got his reasons."

Before I could ask if he was referring to the dog or its owner, the older man got out of the car. I followed suit, grabbed the bag off the backseat and followed him to the front door.

A woman answered the door and smiled warmly as soon as she saw Dr Fields, standing aside to welcome us in. She looked around thirty years old—just a few years older than me—and had brown, curly hair, pale skin, and a wide, kind smile.

"Hannah," Dr Fields introduced us, "this is Dr Carter Reece. Carter, this is Hannah Brannigan."

I extended my hand, which she shook. "Very nice to meet you."

She was still smiling. "Does Max have you doing the rounds with him?"

She called him by his given name, so I quickly deduced she knew him well. Before I could answer, Dr Fields answered for me. "Dr Carter will be taking my place at the hospital."

"Oh," she said quietly, looking from me to the old man.

"You're retiring?" she asked, and Dr Fields nodded. "Isaac never mentioned it…"

"He doesn't know," Dr Fields told her quietly. "I was going to tell him today."

Just then, a man no older than me walked into the foyer. He was dressed as though he'd just stepped off a yacht. Khaki shorts, white polo t-shirt, expensive leather boat shoes and small, dark, designer sunglasses worth what I earned in a month. He was fit looking, matched my five foot ten height and had short, spiky dark brown hair and pale skin. He was gorgeous.

He smiled. "Tell me what?"

*This guy was Isaac Brannigan?* I don't know why I was expecting an old man, but I was. Dr Fields had said Isaac had a caregiver, and I assumed Hannah—with the same surname—was the daughter assigned to such duties. Maybe she was the wife.

"I'll go get Brady," Hannah said, just as Isaac walked out into the foyer. "I let him out for a toilet break before you got here."

Dr Fields smiled at her then turned to face Isaac. The younger man was looking toward me, though not directly at me. "And we have company?"

"Ah, yes," Dr Fields said. "Isaac Brannigan, this is Dr Carter Reece. He's a vet, too."

"Hi," I offered. "Nice to meet you."

"And why's he here?" Isaac asked, rather rudely. I was a little shocked at his blatant rudeness toward me.

"Shall we sit in the living room," the older man said. "I have some news."

Isaac turned and walked through the large opening toward the sofas. He lightly touched the edge, then the arm of the sofa, before he turned and sat down. Dr Fields followed him, while I still stood, a little baffled, in the foyer.

Dr Fields had said this guy was *insistent*. I thought he was just fucking rude. But I followed them anyway and sat on the sofa across from Isaac, while Dr Fields sat next to him. And he did the oddest thing. He put his hand on the younger man's knee.

"I brought Carter along with me today to meet all my house calls," Dr Fields told him, "because he's my replacement. I'm retiring, Isaac."

Isaac just sat there. No reaction, his face stoic. He didn't even take off his sunglasses. "When?"

"In two weeks," Dr Fields said.

Then Hannah walked in from the kitchen to where we were sitting with, who I presumed was, Brady, a golden lab, maybe two or three years old, with bright eyes and a happy face. He trotted in and sat at Isaac's feet as though he was part of this conversation with the humans.

Isaac ignored the dog, which struck me as odd. Not even a quick scratch on the head, not a pat, nothing. Instead, he said, "I'll need some calcium powder. The one I normally get for Brady's food."

Dr Fields nodded. "I thought I brought some with me last time."

"I knocked it over," Isaac said quietly.

Something didn't add up. The way Isaac didn't face Dr Fields square on when they spoke. The glasses. I looked around the room until I found what I was after. Photos on the mantelpiece across the room. And there it was. Photographs of him with another dog. And not just any kind of dog, but with a guide dog.

Isaac Brannigan was blind.

*Blind Faith*

"I'm not sure, Max..." he said. "You've been our vet for so long..."

Dr Fields looked at me and smiled, somewhat apologetically. "Dr Reece is very good. I handpicked him to be my replacement from a slew of applicants. He's moved from Hartford to Boston to take on the position."

"I can understand your reservations," I interjected honestly, and it was then Isaac turned his face toward me. I wanted to prove to him he could trust me, but I figured if I was going to have either Isaac or Brady even begin to like me, I'd have better luck with the dog. So I added, "You trust Dr Fields and you don't know me from Joe, but Isaac, if you don't mind, I'd like to spend a few minutes with Brady."

Isaac mumbled something that sounded like, "Sure, whatever," then stood up and walked toward the open kitchen. Brady sat up taller and he watched Isaac, but didn't follow him.

I called the dog's name softly and he turned obediently to my command. Sitting forward on the sofa, I patted my thigh. "Come."

The dog did as asked, of course, and while he sat between my knees and looked up at me with his big brown eyes, the dog seemed to smile. It made me grin right back at him, and I looked up at Dr Fields, but he was watching Isaac.

The man walked to the edge of the kitchen counter and turned into the kitchen with a familiar ease. He ran his fingers along the countertop and stopped. "Can I get anyone a drink? Iced tea?"

He didn't really wait for an answer; he simply walked over to a particular cupboard, collected glasses, then went to the fridge and pulled out a jug of iced tea.

Obviously familiar in his own kitchen, he did it all as though he could see. I found myself watching him, and it was

7

when Hannah spoke from the sofa beside me, I remembered the reason for our visit.

"Brady's got you figured out," she said with a smile.

I looked down at the dog to find his chin on my knee with his eyes closed, enjoying my absentminded scratch behind his ear. I looked over at Hannah and smiled.

"Yes, I seem to have found a friend."

A rather loud clang from the kitchen made our heads turn. Isaac had dropped a spoon, or from the less than pleased look on his face, I wondered whether he'd done it deliberately. He didn't look happy.

I looked back to Hannah, and she rolled her eyes with a smile. "So, Carter, is it?"

"Yes," I answered, thankful for the distraction. "Carter Reece."

"And you just moved here?" she pressed. "Is that what Max said?"

I nodded, still petting Brady. "From Hartford, but now I call Boston home. I moved into Weymouth, nice and close to work."

Isaac carried a tray of glasses half-filled with iced tea and slowly set it down on the coffee table. I was amazed at how easy he made it look, when I couldn't begin to imagine just how difficult it actually was.

"So, Carter," Hannah said, smiling at me when I finally drew my eyes off her brother. "How's the patient?" she asked, looking to the dog between my legs.

I looked him over, feeling his spine, his hips, ribs, legs and fetlocks. I looked at his eyes, his gums, his teeth, though I really didn't need to. He was a picture of health. But before I could say so, Dr Fields answered. "Brady's what? Nearly three years old now?"

It was a little odd. He wasn't giving any kind of diagnosis. He was steering the conversation. I looked at him quizzically, but he gave a quick but subtle shake of his head and I knew not to question him. But I had to say something. If I wanted Isaac to trust my professional opinion on anything in the future, I had to ask something. So, instead, I asked, "Isaac, how's his appetite?"

It wasn't an invasive question, more of a general observation.

Isaac, who was now again sitting next to Dr Fields, seemed surprised at my question. "He would eat until he exploded if you let him."

I chuckled. Most Labradors, even well-trained guide dogs, would eat until they exploded if you let them, but I didn't say this out loud. "And how many days per week on average does he work?" I wasn't an expert on guide dogs but I knew some. I knew when they were harnessed with their human half of the team, it was called working.

Isaac was still, no expression, no movement, and I wondered if I'd asked a wrong question. But then he answered, "That depends. Sometimes five, sometimes seven days a week." He opened his mouth to say something else, but then obviously thought better of it. He cocked his head in my general direction. "Why?"

"Just getting to know the patient," I answered, hoping he'd hear the nonchalance in my tone. "That's all. I'm sure Dr Fields will fill me in on any particulars if needed."

Dr Fields, my boss for the next two weeks, jumped in on the conversation. "Dr Reece, could you go out to the car and grab the bag of dried dog food? There's a five pound bag in the trunk. I forgot to bring it in."

I could read my cues. He wanted some alone time with Isaac. "Sure."

And as I stood to leave, Hannah joined me. "I'll walk you out."

As we walked out into the warm summer sun, she sighed. "Isaac can be difficult," she said softly. "So don't feel bad. He and Max have known each other a lot of years."

I popped the trunk, collected the bag of dog food and closed the station wagon's rear door. I looked at her and smiled. "I can see that."

She smiled back at me. "You can see which one? That Isaac can be difficult, or that he's good friends with Max?"

I wisely chose not to answer, which was in itself an answer.

Hannah smiled and nodded. "Just don't let him bother you too much. He loves Brady, he does. It's just some days are better than others…"

Before I could ask her what she meant, she looked to the bag in my arms and she brightened. "Come on, I'll show you where you can put that."

We walked back into the house, through the living room where Isaac and Dr Fields were still talking, and into the kitchen. I set the bag of Brady's dry food on the counter and not a second later, the two men in the living room stood, their conversation drawing to a close.

When we were saying goodbye, Dr Fields had taken Isaac's hand, patting it the way a grandfather would his grandson's. "It's not goodbye. I'll call in and see how you're doing from time to time."

Isaac snorted. "If you can drag yourself off the golf course."

Dr Fields laughed. "Well, there's that." But then he grew serious and patted the younger man's hand again. "You can expect the same service from Dr Reece, Isaac. He'll look after you."

Isaac had nodded but did not said anything, and when we'd driven out onto the road, heading back to the clinic, Dr Fields sighed. "Isaac doesn't take change very well," he explained. "He never has."

I thought about that, and what certain changes would mean to a blind man. He was familiar with Dr Fields and he trusted him. Not just in his treatment of his guide dog, but trusted his judgment and also, more importantly, trusted him in his house. His safe haven. Any kind of significant change must be an ordeal.

I looked at the older man and agreed with a nod. "No, I don't suppose he would."

I had questions about Isaac Brannigan, but figured the older man had just basically said goodbye to an old friend, so I decided it could wait another day. We made the rest of the drive back to the clinic in silence and went straight back to appointments. It wasn't until later that evening the questions I had couldn't wait.

I'd finished my daily appointments and was catching up on paperwork when I'd opened the Brannigan file. So I knocked lightly on Dr Fields' office door, and when he looked up, I held up the thick file so he'd know who I was referring to.

"Is there any reason why we run every imaginable test on a healthy dog?" I asked. "Just what exactly are we trying to find wrong with him?"

Dr Fields put down his pen and closed the folder in front of him. He took off his reading glasses, rubbed his thumb and index finger into his eyes and sighed loudly.

"Come in and sit down, Carter," he said, resigned. "Let me tell you about Isaac Brannigan."

## 2

"The first time I met Isaac, he was ten. He was just a boy, learning to deal with being blinded and learning how to live with his first guide dog. Cody, I think its name was, if I remember correctly. It was a while ago now... memory's not like it used to be," Dr Fields shook his head.

I frowned. "*Being* blinded?"

The old man nodded. "He was in a car accident when he was eight. His mother died in the wreck, and he was in the front passenger seat and bore the brunt of the airbag cover."

My stomach dropped. "Oh, God."

Dr Fields nodded again. "It hit him square in the face, apparently. Detached retinas or something like that. Was in a coma, spent a long while in hospital, or so I was told. Lucky to be alive, at any rate."

Jesus Christ.

Dr Fields took a deep breath and exhaled loudly. "They can fix that now, you know," he said with a shake of his head. "Retinal detachment. If they get to it quick enough. But he had fractures," he waved his hand over his face, "everywhere,

*Blind Faith*

and he was unconscious for a long while." He sighed again. "He was just a boy."

He certainly didn't have to explain to me just how much medicine and technology had advanced over the last twenty years. I knew what it was like in the veterinarian sciences, just how different practices and capabilities were now from what they were twenty years ago.

"So," the older man continued, "it wasn't bad enough he had to deal with the loss of his mother, the loss of his sight, but then a few years later, Cody, his guide dog, got sick and passed away. I think Isaac was about fourteen." Dr Fields shook his head. "Poor kid was devastated."

"Jesus," was about all I could say.

Dr Fields nodded. "Then Isaac got a new guide dog, Rosie." The older man smiled. "She was a beautiful dog. A black Lab, smart, strong as an ox. Isaac adored that animal. Loved her. They were inseparable. I think in a lot of ways, that dog replaced a lot of the hurt in his life."

He shook his head and sighed, his smile died. "But Isaac's father didn't cope with the loss of his wife, or the responsibility of a blind son, at all. He drank himself to death; it was a long, slow process, but he died when Isaac was just eighteen." Dr Fields sighed again. "It was Hannah who looked after Isaac all those years. She still does."

This time it was me who sighed. It didn't take a genius to know what was coming next. "And Rosie?"

Dr Fields exhaled slowly. "Rosie was taken out of commission as a guide dog a while before she died. She was old, not too quick, but when her hearing started to go, she posed a safety risk to both of them." He shook his head as he remembered. "Isaac insisted she stay with them regardless. It was about two years before she died, but he refused to even consider a new guide dog until she passed. That was about two years ago."

"Oh, God. How awful."

"Yes," Dr Fields agreed with a knowing nod. "And now he has Brady. Has had him for going on six months."

"He's a fine dog."

"He's a beautiful dog," the older vet added. "But he's no Rosie. At least not to Isaac."

"Is that what he's doing?" I asked. "Trying to *find* something wrong with him?" *Why would he do that? Why would a vet allow it?* "Why are you allowing him to do it?" I asked, not really caring if it sounded rude. "Why enable him and put the dog through that?"

He sighed. "Brady is the most cared for dog I've had the pleasure of seeing. The tests are non-evasive, so I basically give him a fortnightly check-up. I would never do anything to suggest harm to Brady."

I knew this man by outstanding reputation, and I knew he wouldn't harm an animal. And he was right; Brady was in impeccable condition.

"What exactly is Isaac hoping to find?"

Dr Fields shrugged and sighed. "I think he's searching for an excuse, a reason, why he shouldn't have the guide dog."

"It's not compulsory to have a guide dog," I told him. "Isaac had to choose to do this. So if he didn't want the dog, why go through the extensive selection process?"

Dr Fields smiled. "Oh, he wants Brady. With all his heart, he wants that dog. But I think he's keeping him at arm's length because he's terrified of having his heart broken again." The old man smiled sadly. "I guess he figures if he doesn't allow himself to care, he won't get hurt."

I slumped back in my chair. My stomach was in a knot, my voice was quiet. "It's very sad."

*Blind Faith*

"It is." Dr Fields nodded. "I just figured if I played along with it for long enough, and gave him time, he'd realize the problem isn't with Brady."

No, the problem wasn't with the dog. The problem was with the human. It almost always was.

I sighed again. "So I'll be seeing him again in a fortnight?"

Dr Fields nodded. Then he said, "Oh, that's right. He wanted another order of the Calcitrax. He said he'd spilled the last one. Did you want to drop it around to him tomorrow? See what he's like with you when I'm not there."

"Okay," I agreed. "That's probably a good idea. He seemed a little less than pleased with me."

Dr Fields laughed. "Oh, that's just because he didn't know you. He'll warm to you, you'll see."

∼

I'd phoned first and told Hannah I could drop off the powdered calcium for Brady on my way home from work. She'd said it suited perfectly because Isaac worked late on Thursdays. It wasn't until I'd hung up the phone that her words dawned on me. Isaac worked. I'm not sure why this surprised me. It just did.

Actually, the more I thought about Isaac, the more intrigued I was. As I pulled up in front of his house that evening, I wondered what kind of reception I'd get. Taking a deep breath, I grabbed the small canister of Calcitrax for Brady and walked up to the front door. Before I could knock, Hannah opened the door and smiled.

"Hi, Carter. Please come inside."

I walked through the foyer, into the large living room we'd sat in the other day, and headed toward the kitchen. I made a point of showing the powdered calcium to Hannah before putting it on the countertop.

"As requested."

"Oh, thank you," she answered with her usual smile. "We only just got home. Traffic was hell tonight."

Just as I was about to ask where Brady and Isaac where, I heard the familiar clicking of paws on tiles and then a door close. They must have been out in the backyard. Brady walked in first, tail wagging and smiling face. I smiled right back at him.

But then Isaac walked in.

Dressed in a fitted, gray suit and white shirt, with the top button undone, he wore the same designer sunglasses he was wearing the first time I'd met him. My mouth fell open. Jesus. He was good looking dressed in his casual clothes, but dressed in a suit? And a well-fitting suit at that? He looked like he'd stepped off a men's wear catalog. He looked... beautiful.

"Is that you, Dr Reece?" he asked.

I still hadn't shut my mouth, and when Hannah looked at me, I knew that she knew. She caught me staring, ogling, almost drooling over her brother.

"Oh," she whispered, but quickly covered it with, "Yes, he brought the Calcitrax with him." She grinned.

"Yes," I said, clearing my throat, looking to Isaac. "Hope you don't mind me calling in so late."

"No," Isaac replied. "I heard an unfamiliar car and presumed it was you." Then he asked, "What kind of car is it?"

"Oh," I said, shaking my head, trying to get my thoughts back on track. "It's a Jeep four-wheel drive."

Isaac was about to ask another question, but Hannah interrupted. "Why don't you guys go sit down, and I'll bring in something to drink?" Then she put a hand on each of us and pushed us toward the living room. She was still smiling. "Go on," she urged us. "I'll bring it in."

Isaac mumbled some obscenity at his sister, but he did walk over to the sofa and sit down. I followed him, sat down directly across from him, and he wasted no time before the questions started.

"How old are you?"

"Twenty-seven."

"University?"

"UConn," I said. Then I added the full name, "University of Connecticut."

He nodded. "Favorite sport?"

"Ice hockey."

"To watch or play?"

"Watch. I wasn't fast enough to play," I told him with a smile. This interrogation was kind of fun. At least he was talking to me.

"But you can ice-skate?"

"Yes."

"What color is your hair?"

"Black."

"Your eyes?"

"Brown."

"Skin color?"

"What?"

Isaac tilted his head. "Your heritage? Are you black, white, Asian, European?" He pursed his lips somewhat impatiently and didn't give me time to answer. "It's a fair question. You know what I look like, I'd like to know what you look like."

"Would it matter?" I asked.

He laughed, but it wasn't a happy sound. "Why on earth

would it matter what you *looked* like? Why would I care? I can't actually *see* the difference between black and white people, you know. It makes no difference to me." He took a deep breath and started again. "I'm just trying to get a mental image of what you look like."

"I'm white, Caucasian…" I didn't really know how to explain. I've never had to. "I spend as much time outside as I can, so I'm a little tanned."

"What do you do 'outside'?"

"Camping, hiking," I answered. "Well, I used to go hiking back home," I amended. "I haven't had a chance to look around here. But I will."

Isaac nodded, then after a beat of silence, he asked, "Are you married?"

"No."

"Girlfriend?"

I hesitated. "No."

"You hesitated."

I smiled. "Did I?"

"Yes," he answered. "That tells me you either lied, or it's a sensitive subject."

"You'll have to excuse my brother," Hannah said, bringing in two iced teas. She handed one to Isaac. "He has the tact of a wrecking ball."

Isaac shrugged. "Not much point in beating around the bush. I don't have the luxury of seeing facial expressions to gauge one's sincerity."

Hannah snorted. "You also don't have the luxury of manners."

Isaac sighed, and I chuckled as I watched Hannah walk back into the kitchen. They were just as I'd imagined siblings to be. And I found myself fascinated by Isaac. Sure, he was good looking, beautiful even, but it was more than that. He was blind, yes, but he was confident, proud, and even arrogant. It was a barrier he put up around himself, to protect himself. I knew that.

I couldn't help but wonder what the real Isaac Brannigan was like.

His lips twisted thoughtfully, but before he could say anything, Hannah called out from the kitchen, interrupting us. "Carter, will you stay for dinner?"

"Um, I can't," I answered. I stood up and looked at Hannah. "Thank you for the offer, it's very kind. I should get going. I have a very impatient lady at home."

"I thought you said you didn't have a wife or girlfriend at home," Isaac said from the sofa.

I smiled. "The very impatient lady I refer to is a Border Collie-cross called Missy. She's my dog."

"You never said you had a dog," he replied.

"You never asked."

Isaac's mouth snapped shut then he almost pouted. Hannah laughed.

"Something funny, dear sister?" Isaac asked petulantly.

She laughed again. "Yep." Then she turned to face me. "Thanks again for dropping the powder around."

"It was no problem," I answered. "I've rather enjoyed this little interrogation."

"You mean the Spanish Inquisition?" she quipped, walking over to us.

I chuckled again.

Apparently happy to ignore the jibe altogether, Isaac stood and turned to face us. He took a deep breath and squared his shoulders. "Do you have any questions for me?"

Only about a million. But I suddenly didn't want to ask. I didn't want to ruin what we'd accomplished tonight by asking the wrong thing.

"Only one."

He tilted his head, obviously surprised by my answer. Isaac lifted his chin, proudly. Defiantly. "Ask away."

"Did I pass?"

There was a beat of silence. "Pass what?"

"The Spanish Inquisition? The little twenty-question test you just gave me. Did I pass?"

Isaac turned his face away from me. "Maybe."

I grinned, and Hannah silently nudged me with her elbow.

"Then I'll see you next week," I told him.

I don't know why his approval meant so much, but I grinned the entire way home.

# 3

The next two weeks went quickly. Dr Fields was finishing up and I was taking his place, which meant he had a lot of ends to wrap up, and I had a lot to learn. The fundamentals were the same, but it was dealing with different staff, different personalities, different settings, and different routines.

I worked late most nights and when I got home, I took Missy for long walks. It gave me a chance to learn my new neighborhood, taking a new route each night, and it gave me time to wind down after work.

Mark, my best friend back in Hartford, called me, or I called him every few days to trade updates. There wasn't much new happening back home, there never was. Same people, same circles, same shit. But I missed him.

Mark was bi-sexual. His motto was, he wasn't fussy, which translated, meant he'd fuck anything that moved. And he usually did. Except me. We'd met as a blind date a few years ago, a mutual friend of a friend had thought we'd be a good match. We met, hit it off fantastically, but not in a relationship kind of way.

I'd told him I wasn't the one-night stand kind of guy, and he'd laughed, saying he never had to work hard for a fuck. And by work hard, he meant a second or third date. I'd laughed at his brutal honesty, and even though we weren't couple material, we had a lot in common and just clicked.

Four years later and we were as close as friends could be. Without the fucking.

"How's it going?" Mark had asked one night.

I sighed into the phone. "It's all good."

"No regrets?"

It wasn't the first time he'd asked me that. "None."

"Any prospects?" he asked. I could hear the smile in his voice.

My mind leapt straight to Isaac Brannigan, which surprised me. "Not really," I hedged. "Maybe."

"Hmm," he hummed, and I knew his interest was piqued. "Explain 'not really, maybe'."

I sighed again. "One of the receptionists-come-assistants at work tries to flirt with me," I admitted.

"Ooh," Mark replied. "Is he cute?"

"It's a she."

Mark laughed. "That explains the 'not really'."

I chuckled. "Yeah, I guess it does."

"So there's no hot guys coming in to check out the new vet?"

I considered not telling him, but I've never *not* told him anything. I exhaled loudly. "There is one…"

"And?"

"And what?" I asked. "He's gorgeous. But he's arrogant as hell."

"So take him out," Mark said slowly, as though I was stupid. "And fuck the arrogance out of him."

*Blind Faith*

I chuckled into the phone. "You sure do have a way with words."

Mark laughed. "So what's this gorgeous, arrogant guy's deal?"

I shrugged, though he couldn't see. "I don't know. I don't even know if he's gay. I mean, there's been no mention of a girlfriend. No pictures in his house."

"You've been to his house?"

I laughed. "I do house calls."

"You do *what*?"

I laughed again. "House. Calls. You know, like in the old days."

This time Mark laughed. "Jesus. You didn't move to Boston. You moved to the 1920's."

I grinned. "Yeah, Dr Fields is old-school."

"So, will you keep doing house calls when he retires?" Mark asked. "How long 'til he's out of there anyway?"

"He'll be done at the end of the week." I leaned back on the sofa, put my feet up on the coffee table and scratched Missy behind the ear. "And I guess I'll keep doing the house calls. There's only a few on the books anyway. Isaac's one of them."

"Isaac?"

"The gorgeous, arrogant guy," I told him. It wasn't lost on me that I hadn't told him Isaac was blind. I don't know why I didn't. I just didn't.

"So when's the next house call?" He asked suggestively.

"The end of this week," I answered.

"So ask him out."

"It's not that simple."

"Yes, it is. It's exactly that simple."

Everything was exactly that simple to Mark. I sighed, and he knew my side of that argument was over. So he changed the subject. "Well, tell me about this vet's assistant, receptionist, whatever she is. Is she cute?"

I snorted. "How the hell am I a judge of that?" I shook my head. "She's attractive, I guess. For a woman."

"How old is she?"

"Oh, for God's sake, Mark," I laughed into the phone.

"What?" he defended himself. "When I visit next month, I want options."

He'd helped me move here and had planned to give me a month or so to settle in before he came back for a weekend. "You're not doing *anything* with anyone I have to see at work and have to apologize to for your actions, every day of the week."

Mark huffed into the phone. "Hurtful."

I laughed. "Truthful."

He chuckled. "Does Isaac have a sister? A brother?"

"Whoa, just stop," I cried. "You're not going there."

Mark laughed loudly into the phone. He told me he wanted details of my next house call to Isaac's, he told me he missed my sorry face, and he disconnected the call.

I sat there on the couch with Missy almost asleep beside me, and smiled at the dial tone. From all the life I'd left behind in Hartford, I missed Mark the most.

∼

My next house call to Isaac's didn't exactly go as planned. I certainly didn't go there with the intent of asking him out, but that's exactly what happened.

It was a Thursday, and since Isaac worked later on Thursdays, it was already getting dark. He and Hannah had only gotten home about ten minutes before I arrived. Isaac was in a good mood, he even smiled at me when I walked in.

*Blind Faith*

He was just finishing up on a phone call on his cell, so he walked into another room, giving himself some privacy. I greeted Brady with a good pat and when I looked up, Hannah was grinning at me.

She pointed toward the room where Isaac had gone, and whispered, "I have to whisper, because he has impeccable hearing, but I think he likes you."

Before I could respond, or even turn her words over in my head, Isaac walked into the room. "Sorry about that," he said, putting his phone back in his pocket. "Just sorting out details for work next week."

I was almost glad he couldn't see me, because I was still staring, open-mouthed, at his sister.

"Everything okay?" he asked.

Hannah giggled, and I recovered quickly. "Oh, sure. Everything's just fine."

Isaac turned his face toward me. "Did she say something to you?"

Jesus.

Isaac was blind, yes. But he didn't miss a thing.

He turned his face in my direction. "Silences, pauses in conversation... you'd be surprised at how the lack of sight improves other areas of interpretation."

Hannah rolled her eyes and changed the subject. "Isaac, I'll just be finishing up in the laundry, okay?" And with that, she left us alone.

So I checked Brady over, just as Dr Fields had told me to, asking a few questions about his diet and his behavior, which seemed to please Isaac. I noticed he was wearing another well-fitted suit like the one he'd worn the other day, and I wondered where he worked. So while everything was still going well, I decided to ask him some questions.

"Okay, my turn," I said.

"Your turn for what?" he asked quietly, hesitantly.

"For Twenty Questions."

Isaac sighed, and after a few seconds, he frowned. "Okay."

"Are you sure?" I asked. "We don't have to if you don't want to."

"Is that one of your twenty questions?"

"No," I replied. "Should I start again?"

"Jeez, Carter, that's two! You've got eighteen left."

I smiled, and with a laugh, I asked, "Okay, where do you work?"

"Hawkins School for the Blind."

"How long have you worked there?"

"I went there as a student," he explained. "Now I work there."

"What do you do?"

"I teach English, and I'm on the Board."

"Are all the students you teach blind?"

"To some degree."

"That's excellent," I told him. He turned his face toward me quickly, and I realized how my words might have sounded. "No, I mean your job is excellent, not that the students are blind."

"Oh," he said quietly.

Shit. Okay, next question. "How do you get around your house so well? You walk around like you can see."

He almost smiled. "I know where everything is. My mind has this house mapped out."

"That's pretty cool."

He gave me a half smile. "That's not a question."

I found myself smiling back at him. "How do you buy clothes? I mean, you're always impeccably dressed, and… and… "

"...and what?" he finished. "Everything matches?"

I laughed. "Well, yes. Do you just call Bloomingdale's and order their season collection?"

Isaac tried not to smile. "Hannah."

"Hannah what?"

"Hannah orders my clothes for me. She knows what I like, what suits me."

"Um, I don't mean to sound rude, but how do you know what suits you?"

Isaac smiled, but then he shrugged indifferently. "I don't. I can tell which fabrics are which by feeling them, and the quality, but as for color... or what's written on them."

"As in written on your clothes?"

Isaac nodded. "A few years ago, there were a few occasions where I'd, well, I'd pissed Hannah off, and she paid me back."

"Paid you back with what?"

"Well, apparently I've worn Sesame Street and Disney to school."

I looked at Isaac. "Really, Isaac? She did that to you?"

Isaac nodded. "Apparently. Of course I didn't know until I got to school and someone told me the Big Bird shirt I was wearing was so yellow even they could see it, and they only had ten percent vision." Then he added, "She hasn't done it in years though. Well, not that I've known."

I laughed because I couldn't believe it. And then I laughed some more because it was funny.

Isaac scowled at me. "It's not that funny."

"Oh, yes it is," I told him. "What else does she do to you for payback?"

Isaac sighed. "She'll put broccoli on my plate and not tell me."

"And that's bad?"

He screwed his nose up. "Anything that tastes like broccoli is bad."

I laughed again, but he just shook his head and smiled. "You're really not very good at twenty questions, Carter. You've used up nineteen of your twenty and haven't really asked me anything."

"Oh, come on!" I said. "We were having a conversation! That's not fair!"

He smiled victoriously. "You have one more question, Carter. Better make it a good one."

I wanted to ask a lot of things. I wanted to know about Rosie, his guide dog before Brady. I wanted to know what he did for fun, if he had a girlfriend, or preferably a boyfriend. I had no clue if he was gay, and I realized, even if he wasn't, I wanted to know a lot of things about this man. So instead, I asked something else entirely.

"What are you doing on Saturday?"

# 4

When I'd suggested an afternoon at the park, Isaac had said no. When I'd suggested the park two blocks from his house, he'd said no. When I'd added I'd bring along Missy and she and Brady would enjoy the playtime, Isaac had said no.

I'd almost given up, wondering how long it should be before I conceded defeat, when Hannah had walked in and told Isaac to shut up and just go already. Isaac had turned to face her and pursed his lips in protest, but she was having none of it. Hannah had sniped back at him to get out of the house and get some sunshine, telling him it'd do both him and Brady a world of good. Isaac had told her to mind her own business, Hannah had grinned at me and I'd told him I'd be at his place at two in the afternoon.

He'd sputtered and protested, but with Hannah's insistence, Isaac finally relented, and on Saturday, I packed a bag of goodies, harnessed Missy into her seat in my Jeep and headed over to Isaac's.

As I drove to his house, I wondered if we'd—being

Hannah and myself—put too much pressure on Isaac to do something he didn't really want to do.

But when I got there, Brady was already harnessed, and Isaac was dressed and ready to go, looking like the Ralph Lauren-catalog-summer-edition-kind-of-gorgeous. If Hannah bought his clothes, she had impeccable taste. His outfit of cargos and polo shirt, loafers and his trademark sunglasses put my no-name brands to shame.

Isaac had greeted me with a rather aloof hello, as though he was spending the afternoon with me just to humor me, or as if he was doing me a favor. Hannah was there, writing out some sort of grocery list and as she asked Isaac if he could think of anything else he might need from the store, she handed me a piece of paper. Written on it were her emergency contact details and a note at the bottom.

*He's looking forward to today. It's all he's talked about for two days. Don't let him tell you otherwise.*

Isaac paused, for the briefest of moments, then replied, "No, Hannah, nothing else."

Then he turned to me. "I thought you were bringing your dog."

"I did," I replied. "She's outside. I told her to wait at the car. I thought we should introduce her and Brady outside first."

So that's what we did. We walked out to the car where Missy was waiting obediently in the shade of the Jeep, and as Border Collie met Labrador with a sniff and the wag of two tails, all was well between them.

Hannah, with her shopping list in hand, locked the door behind her, and after confirming Isaac had his keys and phone with him, bid us farewell.

Then it was just us.

We walked out of the drive in silence for a little while,

and as I walked with Missy on a leash, I almost forgot Brady was working. It wasn't until we got to the end of the block and Brady stopped, that I remembered he was doing his job.

"There's no traffic," I said. "It's okay to cross." As soon as I'd said the words, I wondered if I should have. I wasn't really up to speed on the protocol. We walked across the street, and as we reached the sidewalk, I said, "Um, should I tell you if it's all right to cross the street? Or is it Brady's job?"

He smirked. "It's fine. You can say that, yes."

I breathed an internal sigh of relief. "Just tell me to shut up if I say something out of line."

Isaac smiled. "Don't worry. I will."

And I had no doubt he wouldn't hesitate to tell me to shut up. Before I could comment, he asked, "What did Hannah give you?"

"Give me?"

"Yes," he said. "When she asked me something about grocery items, she handed you something, did she not?"

Jesus. He really didn't miss a thing. "Um…"

He nodded. "I thought so." He lifted his chin indignantly, but didn't stop walking. "It was a piece of paper, a note?"

I couldn't lie to him. "Yes."

We reached the end of the block and again, Brady stopped. "There's a car coming on our right," I said quietly. We waited for the car to pass and when we'd crossed the street and neared the park, I told him, "The note Hannah gave me… it was a note with her cell number. That's all."

Okay, so it wasn't a complete lie.

He nodded. "I knew it. She must think I'm stupid."

I almost snorted. "Far from it," I said as we walked on the sidewalk alongside the park. "Okay, just down here on our left, about a hundred yards away is a bench in the shade. We can sit there if you like."

"Sure," he answered.

Then I thought about my directions, or lack thereof. "Was that okay, or not clear enough? Just tell me if I don't explain something properly."

Isaac shook his head, and answered politely. "It's fine." Then after a second, he added, "People generally give direction as per the clock face. So the park bench is where on the clock face?"

Oh. "Oh, um, about ten o'clock."

Isaac smiled. "Bench, ten o'clock, one hundred yards. Easy, see?"

I smiled. "Right."

We made it to the bench seat, and I watched as Isaac ran his hand along the back of it, then felt the seat before sitting down. Little things, like the seat actually being there, were something I always took for granted. It amazed me how adept he was.

"Free of bird poop," I told him, jokingly. "I promise."

Isaac chuckled. "Yeah, thanks." He sat down next to me, and Brady sat obediently at his feet.

Missy sat at my feet, keenly looking around the park. There were other people there—families, kids, other dogs. It was a big park, with play equipment for the kids and shaded areas to sit. It was a popular place, nestled into suburbia.

"It's busy here," I said out loud.

"It's always been popular," Isaac said. "Though it's been a while since I was here last."

I wondered if the last time he was here was with his old guide dog Rosie, but it was hardly a subject I wanted to bring up at the beginning of our afternoon.

So I worded it a little differently. "Is this Brady's first time here?"

Isaac nodded, but didn't say anything.

"Well," I hedged, "once he's familiar with how to get here, he'll be fine. You can come here anytime."

"Hmm," was all he replied with, though I got the distinct impression it was unlikely to ever happen.

"Anyway," I said after a few moments silence. "Tell me what you do at work."

"My work?"

"Yes, explain your typical day at work."

He seemed a little taken aback by my request. "Well, I start at about eight-thirty, first class is at nine. I teach English Braille, reading and writing, so there might be theory or exams to prepare for."

"How old are your students?"

"They range from six to sixteen," he answered. "I have different classes for different ages."

"Which do you prefer?"

Isaac sighed. "Depends. We have audio books, but I love it when the younger kids learn to read Braille. It gives them a whole new world to explore, but then I love having the older kids appreciate the classics, ya know?"

I grinned. "Sounds amazing."

"What about you?" he asked. "Why a vet?"

I shrugged. "I love animals. Sometimes I like animals more than humans. They're much less complicated."

Isaac laughed. "I guess they are."

I sighed with a smile. "I never wanted to be anything else."

Isaac was quiet for a while, listening I realized, to the sounds of the park. "I'm just letting Missy off for a run," I said as I unclipped Missy's leash and gave her a command to go play. She did of course, with her nose to the ground, her tail high. I looked at Brady, who sat obediently by Isaac's feet. "Is Brady allowed to play?" I asked. Isaac jerked his head back to face me, though he didn't say anything.

My question obviously threw him. So I quickly added, "Or is he keyed to work for certain time frames? I'm not sure what the procedure is."

Isaac took a deep breath and swallowed. "Um, I guess he can..." he hedged, unsure. Then with hesitant fingers, he undid Brady's bridle and with a simple hand command, Brady looked around before wandering off.

"I won't let him go far," I reassured Isaac. "He's just heading down to the trees with Missy."

Isaac tilted his head. "It's busier here today than I remember it being."

I looked over the park, not taking my eyes off the dogs for too long. "When were you here last?" I asked.

"Oh, a while, I guess," he said quietly. "Over two years ago."

And my suspicions were correct. The last time he was here was with Rosie. "Well," I started, "there's some play equipment that looks new, over there to your right. At about two o'clock," I corrected. "And there's some landscaping along the far boundary at twelve o'clock that looks kinda new."

"There's a gathering of people at about eleven o'clock," Isaac said. "I'd say between five and ten people."

I smiled. "Sure is. Looks like a kids party. They're at the barbecue area."

"There's a barbecue area?"

I chuckled. "So, it's new too."

Isaac smiled, but then he sighed. "Like I said, it's been a while."

"Will you come back? With Brady?" I asked. I watched his face, though his expression rarely changed.

He shrugged. "Maybe."

I didn't want to push him, so I dropped the subject. But then he said, "Wompatuck State Park, out on Route 228, I used to take the bus there. There are some trails I'd walk that front some ponds. The sounds of the water and the birds are amazing."

I thought about that. *I used to take the bus there.* "Wait. You went there on your own?"

He turned his face toward me.

I shook my head, still not really believing it. "You went trail hiking, through the woods and near some lake, by yourself?" I asked again, and he nodded. I laughed, incredulously. "I don't know if you're brave or crazy!"

And then it happened. Isaac Brannigan smiled. Not a smirk, or a smug sneer, but a genuine smile.

And if he was beautiful before, he was something special when he smiled. Outdoors in the filtered sunshine, with the light in his hair and on his face, he was striking. He had perfect teeth and pink lips, and his whole face just lit up.

He was wearing the sunglasses of course, and I wondered what he looked like without them. I wondered if I would ever know.

He was still smiling. "Well, I don't know about brave, and if I were crazy, would I know to admit it?"

I laughed. "I guess not." Then I asked, "Did you really? Go hiking by yourself?"

"At first it was with Hannah or a group from the school, but usually with a sighted person," then his smile died. "I had a dog, of course. And a cane."

I was pretty sure I knew which dog he was talking about, but seeing as though he mentioned it first, I thought it was a window of opportunity to ask.

"A dog?"

Isaac smiled sadly. "Her name was Rosie. She knew every trail, every path." He sighed quietly, and he turned his face away from me.

I could tell the mere mention of his previous guide dog was enough to upset him. His good mood was gone, so I decided to take the emphasis off him.

"I used to go hiking, I think I told you," I said coolly. "Back in Hartford, if I had any time off, I'd head out for the weekends, hike up into the mountains and go camping. It was my world away from the world, if you know what I mean."

Isaac nodded, but didn't say anything.

So I kept on talking. I told him about a few camping adventures I'd had by myself, or the disastrous time my best friend, Mark, decided to come with me. While I was rambling on, I stopped to call the dogs back once or twice—though they never ventured too far—and it wasn't long before I had Isaac back to smiling.

He even asked a few questions about my work, my life in Hartford, and about my friendship with Mark and how we met through mutual friends, but it wasn't too long after that he seemed to grow uneasy. He turned his head as if listening for something in particular.

"Where's Brady?"

"He and Missy are just to our left, about fifty yards away," I told him. "They're still snooping and sniffing, having a grand old time." But I could tell Isaac was a little agitated, so I called the dogs over, took a bottle of water out of my backpack, along with the plastic container, and gave them a drink.

"Do you always carry a water bowl around with you?" Isaac asked, amused.

"Yep," I answered with a grin. "And one for me and one for you," I told him, as I handed him a bottled water. "It's just water," I added. "Not very cold, but something to drink anyway."

Isaac gave me a small smile and a quiet thanks. After he'd had a drink, he handed me back the bottle and said, "I'd like to go home now."

"Yeah, of course," I told him. I watched as Isaac quickly re-harnessed Brady, his fingers feeling the familiar leather clasps and buckles, and it amazed me at just how competent and independent he was. I found myself smiling at him.

"I had a great time this afternoon," I told him. "We should do this again."

Isaac froze, for just a second. "Um…"

I covered quickly with giving Missy a good hard pat. "I think Missy and Brady had the most fun though. I've been so busy with work now that Dr Fields has finished, I've not been able to give Missy as much attention as she's used to, so today's been good for her."

Isaac stood quietly and faced the way we'd come. I took that as our cue to leave. We were halfway back to his house when he asked me if Dr Fields had officially retired.

"As of yesterday."

His voice was quiet. "Oh."

"I'm sure he'll call into the hospital to see how we're all coping without him," I said, trying to reassure him. "I can have him call you if you'd like?"

Isaac's eyebrows knitted together. "It's not that," he said. "I don't want you to think I'm undermining your treatment for Brady."

I smiled. "Isaac, Dr Fields was your friend, yes?"

"Um," he said, unsure. "I guess?"

"Then call him," I told him. "As a friend. Ask him how his golf's going."

Isaac huffed. "What do I know about golf?"

I chuckled. "You don't need to know anything. You just need to listen to him talk about it."

He smiled at that and asked about my work, what I liked, what I didn't, how I found the people. It was easy to talk to him, when he finally decided he wanted to talk, that is. Isaac was a confounding man. He seemed so open, then for reasons only known to him, he'd abruptly snap shut. He was puzzling. He was intriguing.

We arrived at his house and the conversation was going smoothly, until he asked about how I found working with the other staff. "I mostly deal with Rani and Kate when I call," he said. "If I ever had to phone them, or leave a message for Max."

"Oh," I said, leaning against his kitchen bench. "Rani is my assistant, very good, very professional. Kate, on reception, is proficient, but…" I wasn't sure why I was saying this. "But I think she has a bit of a crush on me."

Isaac put Brady's harness on the countertop and turned his face toward me. "Oh. How do you know?"

I chuckled, embarrassed. "She hangs around me, stares at me, giggles, blushes. That kind of thing."

Isaac turned woodenly to face away from me. I tried to gauge his expression but his stoic mask was back in place. "Then you should ask her out."

And this was it. I hesitated for a brief second, wondering if I should or shouldn't tell him I was gay, and in the end, honesty won out. "Well, she's not exactly my type…"

"Why not?" he snipped at me. Isaac scoffed, "Didn't think you'd be the judgmental type, Carter."

His biting tone surprised me. "Pardon?"

"What is it that you don't like about her," he asked coldly. "Is she too blond? Not blond enough? Too tall, too short? You know, judging someone by the way they *look*, is—"

"Jesus, have you finished lecturing me?" I snapped at him, cutting him off mid-rant. "No, I don't judge people by what they look like, thank you very much. And though it's none of your damn business, but if you really want to know why she's not my type, it's because she's female."

I watched the shock on his face, first that I'd stood up to him, and second was the realization of what I'd just told him. Females are not my type. His mouth dropped open then snapped shut again, and the color seemed to drain from his face yet he blushed at the same time.

"Oh," was about all he could say.

I was completely thrown with his hot and cold mood swings and the chip on his shoulder, but as much as I wanted to give him a piece of my mind, I couldn't. He was a customer, a client. And I'd just outed myself as gay to him. So instead, I opted for a quiet truth.

"You criticize me for judging people, Isaac, yet you think you can judge me."

"No, I—" he started, but I didn't want to hear it.

"I'm sorry, Isaac," I said, walking out of the kitchen. "I should go." I collected my backpack, called out for Missy, and let the door close loudly behind me so he'd know I'd left.

Yes, Isaac was baffling, and puzzling and even amazing.

But he was also one fucking moody bastard.

# 5

I was still mad when I got to work the next day. His behavior dumbfounded me. We'd had the best afternoon, and the more time I spent with Isaac, the more I realized I liked him. Not just liked... I admired him.

But his moods turned on a dime, and he had a sting in his temper.

I had no doubt it was a defense mechanism of some sort, and I could understand that. But I had no idea what had changed, what I'd said, what I'd done, what triggered his tirade at me.

I hardly slept a wink because I replayed the conversation over and over in my head, and by morning, I was tired and cranky, and quite frankly, pissed off at him.

I gave up on sleep and took Missy for an early morning walk with hopes of clearing my head. I didn't technically have to work since it was Sunday, but figured I might as well get my head around the animal hospital now that Dr Fields was gone. By mid-morning, I'd done nearly an entire day's work and was feeling pretty good. Tired, but good.

Until Rani put her head around my office door and interrupted me. "Dr Reece?"

"Yes, Rani?"

"Phone call, line two," she said quietly, obviously not sure if I was officially on duty. "It's Isaac Brannigan. I told him you weren't the vet on call today, but he insisted."

Insisted. I bet he did.

I gave Rani a smile. "Thanks. I'll take it."

She left and I stared at the blinking button on the phone. I really had no idea what this phone call would entail, whether he was calling to make a complaint against me, tell me he'd like referrals to another not-gay vet, or apologize.

With Isaac, any of those three options were likely. I sighed when I realized it could very well be all three.

I picked up the handset and pressed the flashing button. "Hello, Carter Reece speaking."

There was a fraction of silence. "Um, Carter, it's Isaac. Isaac Brannigan."

His voice sounded sheepish, even a little sorry. I still played it professional until I knew which way the conversation would go. "Isaac, what can I do for you?"

"I didn't think you were working today," he said. "I've been calling your cell phone, but it just goes to voice mail."

I pulled my phone out of my pocket. "Oh, it was switched to silent," I said absently. There were three missed calls. One last night and two this morning. Then something dawned on me. "Is Brady okay?"

Isaac cleared his throat. "Oh, he's okay," he replied softly. "That's not why I wanted to speak to you."

I took a deep breath and asked the loaded question. "Why did you want to speak to me, Isaac?"

He cleared his throat again and I thought I could hear him fidget, or shift in his seat. "I wanted to apologize."

I still couldn't believe what he'd said. "Apologize?"

"Yes," he lamented. "I was rude to you, and I'm sorry."

"Isaac, it's fine," I told him, though I'm sure my tone said otherwise.

"No, it's not."

"Isaac," I started, but he cut me off.

"Could you come over?" he asked quickly. "I know it's a lot to ask, all things considered, but I'll make lunch. It's the least I can do."

I rubbed my temples. "Um…"

"Around one-ish?"

"You don't hear the word 'no' very often, do you?"

"Uh," he said, as though he had to think about it. "Not very often, no."

I smiled. "Fine. I should be done around one-thirty. See you then." I was still smiling when I hung up on him. I could have been there at his specified one o'clock, but figured I'd make him wait.

~

I arrived at Isaac's and, not entirely sure of what I was walking into, rang the doorbell. Expecting Hannah, I was met by Isaac, who without a word, held the door open and waited for me to walk inside, where I was met by a tail-wagging, happy-to-see-me Brady. I gave the dog a pat then turned to see Isaac closing the door. He seemed nervous.

He looked his usual handsome self, wearing jeans, a t-shirt and his trademark sunglasses. I waited for him to close the door while he took a deep breath and exhaled slowly.

"Please come in," he said quietly. "I put together a lunch. It's in the kitchen."

"It wasn't necessary," I told him as I walked through the living to the open kitchen. "But thank you."

It was awkward. I felt uncomfortable, and still not entirely too sure of the purpose of my visit.

"It's the least I could do," he said. His voice was soft but direct. "I was very rude to you, and I'm sorry."

It was an honest apology, and I couldn't doubt his sincerity. "Apology accepted."

He gave a nod and almost smiled, then turned to the fridge and brought out a platter of cold cut chicken and salad. He placed the platter on the counter then turned again to another cupboard and retrieved two plates. I considered offering my help, but he really had it all under control.

As he put the cutlery down on the counter, I sighed. "Isaac, I need to apologize too."

His face turned quickly toward me. "What for?"

I took a deep breath and exhaled slowly. "Well, for starters, I shouldn't have been talking to you about other staff at the clinic. It was very unprofessional of me. And despite whether Kate has a crush on me, or is or isn't my type, it doesn't matter. The truth is, she's very good at her job and I couldn't do my job properly without her."

Isaac's face flinched as though he didn't agree. "It's certainly not your fault. I brought the subject matter up."

"Yes, but still," I conceded, "I shouldn't have said anything."

"Well, I accept your apology, though I don't entirely agree with it," he said defiantly.

I shook my head. Of course he didn't agree with it, I thought. The word incorrigible came to mind. It didn't take long to figure out that Isaac rarely thought he was wrong, and I wondered just how much it hurt him to apologize to me. It made his apology just a little more meaningful.

Isaac handed me an empty plate and waved his other hand toward the chicken salad. "Please, help yourself."

"Sure," I answered, and filled his plate too. As I handed his lunch back to him, I said, "And I should apologize for… well, for telling you that women were not my type."

He put his plate down on the countertop. He opened and closed his mouth, then a light blush crept over his cheeks. "Don't apologize for that," he said quietly. "I'm glad you told me."

He was glad I told him?

Before I could respond, he quickly changed the subject. "There's a jug of water in the fridge, can you get it for me?"

"Of course," I told him and did as he asked, while he got two glasses out of the overhead cupboard to his right. I poured two glasses of water and, putting one in front of him on the countertop, I took his left hand and gently wrapped his fingers around the glass.

He blushed, and his voice was barely a breath. "Thank you."

And it clicked into place. He was glad I told him I didn't like women, he blushed when I touched his hand, Hannah telling me he liked me. As in *liked me*, liked me.

Figuring I had nothing else to lose, I took a deep breath and asked, "Isaac, are you gay?"

His face jolted around toward me, shocked at my blatant question, then he blushed a deep scarlet. I didn't give him time to be embarrassed. Instead, I chuckled. "So, seeing anyone?"

"Not for the last eighteen years," he deadpanned.

"Oh, shit," I cried, as I realized what I'd just said to a blind man. "I didn't mean seeing as in *seeing*, I meant *seeing* as in seeing someone."

*Blind Faith*

Isaac laughed at me. "Oh, that makes sense," he said with a sarcastic laugh. "You mean as in dating?"

"Yes, dating!" I cried. "Shit, I'm sorry."

Isaac laughed again. "It's fine, Carter, really. I was just kidding. You're allowed to say things like 'you should have seen it' or 'are you seeing anyone.' I'm not offended by that."

I exhaled, relieved. "Jeez, I'm sorry," I told him again.

He grinned at me. "Stop apologizing and have a drink of water," he suggested. "It might help wash that foot down."

I rolled my eyes at him, though of course he couldn't see it. Still smiling, he pushed his plate across the bench top, then walked around me, pulled out a stool from under the kitchen bench and sat down.

"We can sit at the dining table, if you'd prefer?"

"No, this is fine," I told him, and pulled out the stool next to his and sat down for lunch.

Isaac had a few mouthfuls, then said, "And the answer to your question is no."

"No?"

"No, I'm not dating anyone."

Oh.

"Are you?" he asked, before he took another mouthful of lettuce and tomato.

I swallowed my food and took a sip of water. "No, not for a while," I admitted. "There was a guy for a while, but that ended about a year ago."

Isaac nodded, playing it cool. "What was his name?"

"Paul."

"Why'd you break up?"

Jeez, he wasn't shy on asking point-blank questions. "Um, we wanted different things." That was a diplomatic way to put it.

"What kind of things?" Isaac pressed on. "Career, family?"

I speared a cherry tomato with my fork. "He wanted to sleep with other people apparently."

The fork in Isaac's hand stopped halfway to his mouth. "Oh."

I chuckled at his expression. "Yeah, it wasn't pleasant."

"Oh," he said again. He took another mouthful of chicken and chewed thoughtfully. "Is that why you moved here, and took on the new job?"

I shook my head, but then remembered I had to say the word out loud for him. "No. No, not at all. Like I said, it all happened a year ago. I was over that ordeal long before this job came up, but when it did, I thought it was the perfect time to move on with my life."

"Fair enough," he agreed.

"What about you?" I asked again. "Ex-boyfriends?"

He shrugged. "Not for a long while." Then he amended, "I used to spend time with a guy in school. I guess you'd say it was dating."

"What was his name?" I asked. He looked hesitant so I added, "Fair's fair, I told you mine."

He smirked. "Daniel."

"What happened to Daniel?"

"They moved away," Isaac said. "We were young and not sure what we wanted, really."

I smiled. "You just fooled around and experimented?"

Isaac's mouth fell open then promptly snapped shut. He shrugged, "Mmm, maybe."

I chuckled at him. "Does Hannah know?"

Isaac finished the last of his salad and nodded. "Yes, of course. I can't hide much from her."

I found myself smiling. "Where is she?"

"At her house."

I had to think about that for a second. "Doesn't she live here with you?"

"No," Isaac said, shaking his head slowly. "She used to, but she got married last year, and now has her own place. Her husband, Carlos, is a really nice guy."

"You live here by yourself?" I asked, incredulously. "Is that safe?"

He lifted his chin and spoke as though he'd had this conversation a thousand times. "It's perfectly safe. Hannah is here from breakfast 'til dinner every day except Sundays. I have the best security system, this place gets locked down at night, and I'm a grown man. I'm an adult, twenty-six years old, I'm allowed to live by myself."

"I didn't mean to offend you," I told him sincerely. "It just amazes me how independent you are, how proficient you are at doing stuff, at looking after yourself." I huffed and shook my head. "Jesus, I'd be hopeless."

"Well, I didn't really have a choice," he told me. "I could have either crawled into a hole and died, or got on with my life."

I shook my head. "You're an amazing man, Isaac."

He shrugged one shoulder, and I could tell he didn't believe me. After a moment, he pushed his plate away. "Carter, can I tell you something?"

"Sure."

He took a long second, as though he was trying to get the words right in his head before he spoke. "I live here alone, and I'm completely blind," he said quietly. "So I'm sure you can appreciate how difficult it is for me to just invite people in."

I nodded, then again, remembered I had to say my words out loud. "Of course."

Isaac spoke softly. It was the most vulnerable I'd ever seen him. "I know Max, Dr Fields, said I could trust you to come into my home and to look after Brady, but I wanted you to know I *do* trust you. You took me to the park yesterday, which is the nicest thing someone's done for me in a long time, then I wrecked it by yelling at you. I'm so sorry I did that. I didn't mean to... I just..." he trailed off with a shrug. "Anyway, I just wanted you to know, well, yesterday when you said you'd like to go to the park again sometime, well, I'd like that too."

I smiled and opened my mouth to speak, but he was on a roll.

"That's only if you want to," he said quickly. "I wouldn't blame you if you'd rather just keep to professional visits; that's fine too. And just because we're both gay doesn't mean anything, I didn't tell you I was gay to imply, or suggest..."

I smiled at his ramblings. It was kind of adorable.

"I just thought I'd let you know I understood, and I certainly don't have a problem with it. I didn't want you to worry, thinking I'd be offended or want to change vets or something—"

I was still smiling. "Isaac," I interrupted.

He turned his face toward me and waited.

"Shut up."

His mouth fell open. "You're smiling, aren't you?"

"Yes," I said with a laugh. "I'd love to go back to the park," I told him. "I had a really good time."

His lips twisted in a smiling pout. "You told me to shut up."

I laughed again. "Yes, yes, I did."

"Do you tell people to shut up often?" he asked, trying not to smile.

"If it's warranted."

"Right," he said with nod. "I don't think I've ever been told to shut up."

I laughed. "I thought as much."

He smiled shyly. "So, this Saturday?"

I was grinning by now. "I'll check what the weather's doing, but how about we pack a lunch? We can take the dogs."

"I'll organize the food for us," Isaac said. "You worry about the dogs."

"Sounds good."

Isaac nodded. "Yes, sounds good."

It was quiet for a moment between us, though we were both smiling. "Hey, where's Brady?" I asked.

"Oh, he's in the back room," he told me. "Did you want to see him?"

"Sure!" I said.

"Have you had enough to eat?" he asked. "I wasn't sure what you liked."

"It was perfect," I told him as I cleared away the plates, placing them in the sink. "Did you make it?"

Isaac nodded. "Yeah, Hannah usually preps a lot of my food or leaves it pre-cooked and I just have to reheat, or she'll cut it up for me. Like the chicken, mostly bite size so I don't have to worry about cutting or biting into something that's too big, especially in front of other people."

It was little things like that that I didn't give a second thought to. "Well, you did well. It was good, thank you."

Isaac smiled and walked around the bench into the kitchen. "Please leave the dishes. I'll do them later. Let's go find this dog."

He turned and walked through the door at the back of the kitchen. I'd seen Hannah take laundry through that door, so I figured it went outside. I followed him through the door and found myself in a large sunroom. There was a door to the right, which I could see was a laundry room, but the sunroom itself was beautiful.

There were white cane chairs and a matching table setting, large potted succulents and cyclamens. The back wall was mostly windows, overlooking a large, manicured lawn and lap pool.

And a golden Labrador lying on his bed. His tail started thumping out a happy beat when he realized we were walking over to him. He had a happy face, bright eyes. He seemed to smile.

"Hey, Brady," I said, kneeling down and greeting him with a good pat. Isaac stood back a few feet, and the cool distance he put between himself and his dog was very clear.

"Can we take him out the back?" I asked. "Let him have a run around?"

Isaac hesitated. "Okay."

It was unsettling how standoffish Isaac was with Brady. The dog was very well looked after, but there was no general affection, no pats, no scratches behind the ear or rubs on the belly. It was sad. As a vet, it bothered me. Unfortunately, I couldn't professionally do anything about it; it was not a criminal offense to not be emotionally attached to an animal. He was well cared for, well provided for. I remembered Dr Fields saying he'd just hoped the attachment would come in time.

We stood in the backyard and talked some more, while Brady sniffed, peed, and sniffed some more. Instead of talking about Brady, I asked Isaac if he swam often and he told me he did, at least once, sometimes twice a day. He had a spare bedroom set up as a gym, apparently, and liked the cross-trainer and stair-master to help him stay fit. No wonder he looked so trim.

"Do you work out?" he asked.

"Uh, not really," I admitted. "I used to have a gym membership, back in Hartford, but haven't got around to finding a new place yet. But I walk a few miles with Missy most nights."

"Would you say you're fit?" he asked. Then he added, "I'm just trying to get a mental picture of what you look like."

Oh. "Um, yeah, I'd say I'm pretty fit. I won't be doing any triathlons any time soon, but I'm okay." I wondered if that was descriptive enough, but realized it probably wasn't. So I told him, "I'm five-ten and a hundred and fifty-five pounds."

Isaac nodded thoughtfully and smiled. "What do you look like?"

I frowned. I'd been told once or twice I looked a little like Colin Farrell, but there was no point in admitting that, because Isaac would have never seen him either.

"Um, I don't know. Just average, I guess."

Isaac was quiet for a long moment, but I could see he was thinking by the way his forehead creased between his eyebrows, just above his glasses. "May I touch your face?" he asked.

I looked at him, stunned at his request. *What? Touch my face?*

Isaac kind of smiled, obviously a little uncomfortable, or nervous. "It's how I see, for the lack of a better word, what you look like. Your eyebrows, nose, jaw… lips."

I swallowed. "Uh, sure."

I was standing close enough to him, so I turned to face him front on. He lifted his hand slowly, and I took his hand, placing it on my cheek.

And I almost stopped breathing.

He lifted his other hand, and soon, his fingers were in my hair. "Your hair is black, yes?"

"Yes."

"It's kind of spiky and soft at the same time."

I smiled. "Yeah, I keep it short because it grows in all different directions."

He tilted his head, and his fingers traced my forehead, my eyebrows. My eyes closed as his fingertips mapped out my eyebrows, eye sockets and temples. "Your eyes are brown; you've told me that."

"Yes," I whispered. "They're dark brown, almost black."

"I pictured you with blue eyes."

My eyes stayed closed, but I smiled. "Sorry to disappoint."

His voice was soft and close. "I'm not disappointed."

Then his fingers traced along my jaw and my chin, and finally, my lips.

My breaths were shallow and my heart was hammering so that I wondered, with his improved hearing, if he could hear it. His fingers were feather-light, touching, tickling on my mouth, my skin. My eyes opened slowly and I watched him lick his lips.

He whispered, "You have soft lips."

I was leaning toward him. I wanted to kiss him. I wanted to kiss him so bad, I could almost taste him. But I couldn't.

I shouldn't.

Fuck, I wanted to.

He licked his lips again and I bit back a moan.

He traced his thumb across my bottom lip, and I leaned in just a little farther. I could feel his breath on my face and then his hands moved to cradle my face. I wasn't going to kiss him.

He was going to kiss me.

And then Brady huffed loudly at our feet.

Startled, Isaac pulled back quickly and looked down to

the sound of the dog. I exhaled loudly, smiling, dazed and out of breath. I gave Brady a pat on the head. "I think he was curious, that's all. Wondered what we were doing."

"Oh," Isaac said, taking a step backward, putting some distance between us.

I shook my head. Jesus. I've had moments before, but never as intense as that. "I should be going," I said as lightly as I could manage. "How about we get you two inside, and you can lock up and set the alarm for the night."

Isaac nodded, then ran his hand through his hair, seemingly as dazed as me. "Good idea."

I took a deep breath. "We're still on for Saturday?"

"Sure."

"Good," I said. "I'm looking forward to it."

"Me too."

## 6

Isaac phoned me Thursday night, and when I saw his name come up on my phone, I thought for a brief moment he was calling to cancel. I said hello, and waited for the words.

Instead, he said, "I was thinking of doing French bread sandwiches for lunch on Saturday. Do you prefer beef, ham, chicken, or just salad?"

I laughed, relieved.

"Something funny?"

I grinned and chuckled into the phone. "No, not at all. Isaac, I eat everything."

"Everything?"

"Yep."

"Shall I organize duck pate and smoked roe?"

"Uh, well," I cringed. "Okay, so maybe I don't eat *everything*."

I could just picture him smiling victoriously. "So, will it be beef, ham, chicken or salad?"

"Ham *and* salad."

He sighed. "You like to challenge me, don't you?"

I grinned. "Yes." Then I said, "Do you have whole grain mustard? Or Dijon mustard for that sandwich?"

He sighed dramatically. "Don't get too carried away, Carter, I'm not a short-order cook."

I laughed. "I'm sure you'll make the best sandwiches ever."

"I don't know," he said playfully with a click of his tongue. "I might get the mustard mixed up with the wasabi."

I gasped. "You wouldn't!"

This time he laughed. "Depends on how much grief you give me."

"Right," I said with a laugh. "Let me just make a note," then I pretended to read out loud what I was pretending to write, "give Isaac lots of grief, but pack plenty of water to wash down wasabi."

He chuckled, and with a sigh, he was quiet. So I asked him, "How was work?"

And he told me what he did that day, what he'd done that week. He spoke with an enviable enthusiasm about his work, his students. Not that I didn't love my job, I did love it, but I think the rewards Isaac got from his job far surmounted mine.

I told him about my day and my week. How I'd treated dogs and cats of all breeds, shapes, and sizes, rabbits, ferrets, gerbils, and birds. Isaac seemed fascinated with my story, and it was only when my phone beeped with another incoming call that I realized Isaac and I had been talking for almost an hour.

"Hey, I better take this call," I explained. "It will be Mark. I was supposed to call him, but didn't realize the time."

"Oh, no worries," Isaac replied. "I guess I better get organized too. I have to go check if we have wasabi, I mean, mustard."

I laughed. "I'll be at your place at bit before twelve."

He chuckled quietly into the phone. "Good. Don't be late," he said, and the line clicked softly in my ear.

I was grinning when I pressed the answer button. "Hello?"

"Where the hell were you, and why do you sound so friggin' happy?"

Ignoring his so-called greeting, I asked, "Hey Mark, how are you?"

"I'm super," he answered brightly. "So, where the hell were you, why did it take so long for you to answer the phone, and why do you sound so friggin' happy?"

I laughed again. "If you really must know, I was on another call."

"Who's more important than me?"

I shook my head and rolled my eyes. "Absolutely no one. God forbid we bruise that ego."

Mark laughed. "So who were you talking to?"

I groaned. He wasn't going to let this go. "Isaac."

"Oh, loverboy," he said in a very mature, sing-song voice. "How is he in bed?"

I sighed. "It's not like that."

"But he's gay, and you like him?"

"Well... yeah..."

"And you haven't fucked him?" he asked bluntly. "You've been talking about him for two weeks now."

"It's different," I offered. "He's different. He's not like other guys."

"Jesus Christ, Carter," Mark said with a sigh. "You're a disgrace to gay men everywhere."

I chuckled at my best friend and his way with words. But I knew I should tell him. He was right, I did like Isaac. And so my best friend should know the truth.

"Mark, there's something you should know about Isaac."

Mark was quiet for a moment and I knew I had him intrigued. "What's that?"

"Well, he's blind."

Silence.

"Blind?"

"Yes," I said slowly. "As in without the ability to see."

More silence.

Then he snorted out a disbelieving laugh. "Are you being serious?" He didn't give me time to answer. "Jesus, you're being serious."

"Mark, I told you he was different," I explained. "But he's smart, funny, very clever."

"And blind!"

"I don't see it like that," I started, and immediately regretted my choice of words.

"Neither does he, apparently."

"Mark, no blind jokes, please."

"Oh, my God," he said quietly. "You really like this guy. And he's really blind?"

"He is," I conceded. "He has a guide dog, Brady. That's how we met. Isaac's on my house call list."

More silence.

"Jesus, Carter, and you're just telling me this now?"

"Well, we're not officially going out or anything; we're not dating," I defended myself. "I've been to his house a few times, we spent some time together last weekend, and now we have a lunch date—" I stopped, then corrected, "a lunch *thing* this Saturday. I wasn't even sure if it would lead to anything. I'm still not."

"But you want it to?"

"Well… yeah, maybe…"

"Then you need to make it happen."

And just like that, Mark was cool with it. Once he knew it

was what I wanted, he wanted me to have it. That was Mark, loyal to a fault.

Our conversation went to things back in Hartford and old friends and work, then when we were saying goodbye, he told me he wanted to meet this Isaac fellow. And in three weeks when he visited for the weekend, he fully expected to.

I told him it would depend on how things went this weekend. "Anyway, I don't think he's ready to meet you just yet."

"Oh, please," he said petulantly. "He'll love me. Everyone loves me."

I rolled my eyes and sighed. "Do you promise to be on your best behavior?"

"Yes," he said with a laugh. "Scout's honor."

"You were never a boy scout."

"No, but I've fucked plenty of guys who were." Then he added, "They were scouts when they were kids, that is. Not now, 'cause that'd be gross."

I laughed. "Goodnight, Mark."

~

"**M**ark wants to meet you."

We were sitting at a park bench and Isaac turned to the sound of my voice. "What?"

"Mark, my best friend," I explained. "He wants to meet you."

"Oh." He looked away from me, then after a long moment, he said, "You told him about me?"

"Sure. I tell him everything."

Isaac nodded slowly. "Oh. What did you tell him?"

"That we were taking the dogs to the park and having lunch."

I couldn't be sure, but I think Isaac was trying not to smile

*Blind Faith*

as though he liked the idea of me talking about him. But then his smile faded.

"Did you tell him about me?" he asked. "You know, being blind?"

I didn't tell him I only *just* mentioned it to him, but I answered honestly, trying to sound like it was no big deal. "Sure."

Isaac's expression gave nothing away. It rarely did. "And?"

"And what?" I asked rhetorically. "And nothing. If I don't mind, then he doesn't either."

Isaac seemed to think about that for a little while. "And you don't mind?"

"Nope."

He tried not to smile. And failed.

We ate our lunch, sans wasabi, and the dogs played, rolled in the long grass, and snoozed by our feet. We must have spent two hours talking about nothing and everything. Well, I did most of the talking, Isaac mostly listened and laughed. He seemed enthralled with my childhood stories, college stories, and then my stories of Mark's antics. He looked carefree, sitting there with me in the sunlight, laughing.

He was still standoffish toward Brady, never patting him, never rewarding him, barely even acknowledging him. I was tempted to say something, but didn't want to ruin the mood.

So I included Brady as much as I could, just like I did with Missy. I didn't overdo it though. I didn't want Isaac to see through me. No, he couldn't see, but he was incredibly perceptive, and he certainly wasn't stupid.

As a vet, I'd seen some pretty heinous acts against animals. But this certainly wasn't any kind of physical misdemeanor, I didn't really know what to class it as. Brady was in better than perfect health, extremely well cared for and had a diet better than most humans. But his owner, his human partner in their dynamic duo, showed no affection, no appreciation.

And Isaac wasn't uncaring. He wasn't a cold-hearted bastard. He wasn't. He was far from it. So while he'd shut himself off from any emotional attachment with Brady to save himself from heartache, I wondered just how futile it was.

Because he did love him. I knew he did. It was there, under the surface. I guess he just figured by telling himself if he didn't show any affection to Brady, he wouldn't allow himself to feel anything.

So as tempted as I was to say something, I didn't. I was having the best day. Actually, it was the best date—if that's what it was—I'd had in a really long time. I didn't want to risk upsetting him. I wanted to stay there all afternoon.

But unfortunately, the weather didn't want to cooperate. "We'll have to get going soon," I told him.

Then he did the oddest thing. He checked his watch. I'd seen he wore one, but I very stupidly didn't give it another thought. Everyone wore watches, but not everyone was blind. He didn't look at it, of course, but he felt it.

"What kind of watch is that?"

"A Braille watch." Then he lifted the glass dial cover and felt the face of his watch. "I read it," he said. "Did you want to see it?"

"Sure."

Then he held his arm out, offering it to me, so I took it. I wrapped my fingers around the side of his hand to look at his watch. I probably couldn't tell you what the watch looked like. I think it was blue or silver, with raised dots instead of numbers. Well, at least I think it was. Because as soon as I had his hand in mine, I forgot what I was supposed to do with it.

All I could think of was that I was holding his hand.

I was touching him. And I knew right then I wanted to touch him again. I wanted him to touch me.

I wanted more of everything with him.

I wanted to talk with him about all sorts of things. I wanted to see him use his hands to explain something when he talked so passionately about his job. I wanted to make him laugh. I wanted to hold his hand, touch him. I wanted to know what he felt like, what he felt like under my touch, what he felt like against me.

I wanted to know him.

I wanted him to know me.

I wanted to understand him. I wanted to get under his skin.

Like he was getting under mine.

"Carter?"

"Mmm, yeah?" I looked at him, then to my hand still holding his. "Oh." I dropped his hand. "There's a storm coming," I told him, changing the subject.

Isaac cleared his throat. "Yes, the wind's picked up."

I looked around at the park, at the trees blowing, the leaves rolling across the grass. "Yeah, we better head back." I collected the dogs' water and treats and packed them into my backpack while Isaac harnessed Brady. "Come on, we'll take a shortcut through the park."

As we started back, I realized the path I'd chosen wasn't exactly flat. "There's a bit of a slope up here, and some trees."

"Oh," Isaac hesitated. Then he reached out his free hand, finding my arm and his hand slid over my forearm, using me as a guide. "Is this okay?"

He looked a little smug, and I grinned. "Yeah, of course."

I was pretty sure he didn't need my guidance, he had Brady after all, but I certainly didn't object. And I was pretty sure he didn't need to leave his hand on my arm the entire way home, but he did. And I smiled the whole way.

When we got back to Isaac's, Hannah offered to take both dogs into the yard with her. She was just finishing up doing laundry, she said. But she was looking between us, and she grinned at me before hurrying out of the kitchen with Missy and Brady, leaving us alone.

"Can I get you a drink?" Isaac asked, heading toward the fridge. "Cold drink, soda, coffee, water?"

I ran my hand through my hair. "Um, maybe later," I said, realizing it implied I'd still like to be there later. "Listen, Isaac," I started, and he stopped, only to walk back to the countertop and stand next to me in the kitchen. From the look on his face, I'd say he was expecting me to tell him goodbye. "I had a really good time today," I told him quietly.

He looked down to the floor between us. "But?"

He was expecting a thanks-but-no-thanks, and his disappointment was clear. Which meant he liked me. I smiled, but before I could answer, he spoke again.

"But I'm what?" he asked flatly. "Not your type? Too much hard work? Too blind?"

And there it was. His temper. His I'll-hurt-you-before-you-can-hurt-me tactic.

I smiled and shook my head. "No, Isaac," I replied softly, putting my hand on his arm. "I was going to say, I had a really good time today *and*—see that was an 'and', not a 'but'—*and* I'd like to do it again."

"Oh."

"Yeah, so put your fuck-you attitude on ice, okay?" I asked with smile. "At least until the second date, all right?"

His lips twisted into an almost-smile. "My fuck-you

attitude?"

I chuckled, but, keeping my hand on his arm, I moved a little closer to him and spoke a little lower. "Yes, the one where you push people away."

He could tell I'd stepped in closer to him. He kept his face down, but his cheeks tinted with a blush and he swallowed. "I don't mean to push people away," he said softly.

"Isaac," I all but whispered. I was standing closer now. I almost breathed the words. "Don't push me away."

He didn't reply in words, but he shook his head just a fraction. I could see the rise and fall of his chest as he took nervous breaths. But he didn't move away, so I slowly brushed my hand up his arm.

"Is this okay?" I whispered.

He nodded.

I moved my feet in a little closer to his, bringing our bodies even closer, and my other hand touched his other arm.

"Is this okay?"

He nodded again.

I licked my lips. I wanted to kiss him. I wanted to know what his lips felt like, what he tasted like.

"Isaac," I murmured, "can I kiss you?"

He swallowed hard, and after a long second, he nodded. So he could feel my hands on him at all times, I slid both hands up his arms to his neck and jaw. I cradled his face, lifting his chin and oh so slowly, my eyes fluttered closed as I leaned in to kiss him.

"Oh, holy shit!" Hannah cried out from beside us in the kitchen. She had a basket of washing in her hands.

Isaac and I took a reflexive step back from each other, and, although I was disappointed and embarrassed, I found myself smiling at Hannah's awkwardness. She still had the basket of laundry in her hands but was now facing the fridge.

"Oh, crap," she said. "I ruined it, didn't I? Shit, shit, shit! I'm sorry."

"You're still ruining it," Isaac mumbled, and I could imagine him rolling his eyes behind his sunglasses.

I laughed. "It's okay, Hannah."

Isaac turned his face toward me with an expression that clearly said *what do you friggin' mean, it's okay?* I chuckled again.

"No, it's not okay," Hannah said quickly, and started backing out of the room. "Oh God, I'm sorry. I just walked in. I wasn't even concentrating on where I was going, then I was right there and you were just about to... oh God, I'm so embarrassed."

She mouthed *I'm sorry, I'm sorry* as she continued to walk backward out of the kitchen, and with a final apologetic cringe, she was gone.

"Well, that ruined that," Isaac mumbled to the floor.

I laughed, and without hesitating, I stepped right in front of him, cupped his face in my hands and kissed him.

He froze for the briefest of moments, but when I moved my lips against his, he relented and started to kiss me back. It was a soft first kiss, gentle and slow. His lips were warm and wet and his hands found my sides. I didn't move to deepen the kiss, but I held his face and moved our lips, keeping it sweet.

It took my breath away.

I slowly pulled my lips from his, keeping our faces close. I could see through the dark lenses of his glasses that his eyes were closed. His lips were parted and glistening, his hands were now fisting my shirt at my sides and he was breathing hard.

I smiled. "Was that okay?"

Isaac licked his lips and nodded, though he still looked a

little dazed. He let go of my shirt, I took his hand and asked him, "Do you want to sit on the sofa?"

He nodded again, so still holding his hand, I led him to the living room and just as we sat down, Hannah called out from the back sunroom. "Can I come in?"

Isaac groaned and I chuckled, calling back to her, "Yes, Hannah, it's fine. We're in the living room."

"There's a storm coming," she told us as she walked into the room with both Missy and Brady at her sides. "So I've brought these guys inside. I'll be heading off now, okay?"

"That's fine, thank you," Isaac said.

"Carter, will you be staying long?" she asked. She wasn't being nosey. Her concern, first and foremost, was for her brother.

I answered, "Yeah, I'll be here for a little while yet."

It was then she looked down at Isaac's hand, still joined with mine, and she grinned. "Okay, that's so great," she said, almost shaking with excitement. She did a weird little happy-dance, and, grinning the whole time, grabbed her bag off the kitchen countertop. "Okay, Isaac, dinner is in the fridge and your Braille template is on the coffee table. I'll call you tomorrow." And with another radiant smile and happy-wiggle, she was gone.

Isaac groaned and sighed, but he was smiling. "Did she do that odd jumpy-wriggle dance?"

I folded my leg under my other thigh and turned my body toward his so I sat facing him and laughed. "Twice."

"Ugh." Isaac groaned again with a laugh and leaned toward me, laughing off his embarrassment.

I lifted his face in my hands and kissed him again. It wasn't lost on me that we were finally alone. "So Isaac, what did you want to do?"

## 7

Scrabble.

Not exactly what I had in mind when I'd asked what he wanted to do, but after he'd kissed me senseless and I'd reciprocated in kind, we needed to slow it down. It was either make out until we were both hot, bothered, sticky messes, or take some deep breaths and sit on opposite sofas. So we opted for the safer, less messy option.

Kissing Isaac, being kissed by him, was wonderful, but it was all too much too soon. So sitting on the sofa across from him, getting my ass kicked in Scrabble was how we spent the afternoon. The dogs slept on the rug near us while the rain poured down outside.

I didn't even know there was a Scrabble game made for the blind. Monopoly, too, apparently, and cards and dominos. Maybe I'd have better luck with a different game, because he was killing me in Scrabble.

"What the hell kind of word is muzjiks?" I cried. "That is so not a word!"

"It is so!"

"Prove it!" I dared him. "Use it in a sentence."

Isaac held up his hand. "Wait here," he said, and walked out of the room. Half a minute later, he walked in, sat down and tossed a dictionary at me.

I caught it, and looked at him disbelievingly. "You know, you've got pretty good aim for a blind guy."

He laughed. "Just look up the word."

I noticed a Braille label on the front of the book, but the book itself was printed words. I flicked through to 'M'. Bloody hell. Muzjiks. A Russian peasant. Of course it was a word. Fuck. A one hundred twenty-eight point word!

"You're killing me here."

Isaac laughed, and I told him, "Tomorrow we can play Monopoly, and then I'll kick your ass."

Isaac's smiling mouth fell open. "You'd do that to a blind guy?"

I laughed. "After the ass-kicking you've given me today, it would only be fair."

He gave me a small, hesitant smile. "Tomorrow?"

I got up and stepped around the coffee table to sit down beside him so I was facing him, and took his hand again. "I'd like that," I told him. "If the weather's good, we can go back to the park, or just go for a walk, and if it's still raining, I'm sure we can find something to do inside."

Isaac kind of froze and I didn't realize how my words had sounded, or what they implied. "Oh, I didn't mean it like that," I added quickly. "I didn't mean to suggest *those* kind of indoor activities."

Isaac bit his lip and pulled his hand from mine. "Carter, there's something you should know."

I waited for him to continue, but he didn't. So I prompted him. "What's that?"

"I, um," he started, then cleared his throat, wiping the palms of his hand on his thighs. "I uh, I've never done anything really, with a guy—with anyone, I should say. I've never, well, I've never been *intimate*..."

When he told me his last boyfriend was basically in high school, I presumed as much. I took his hand off his leg and gave it a squeeze. "Isaac, I don't care about that. I like you, I like spending time with you. We can go as fast or as slow as you like."

A faint color crept over his cheeks. "Oh."

I smiled, but figured if we were going for honesty, it was my turn. "There's something you should know about me," I told him. "My friend Mark thinks I'm a disgrace to all gay men."

"Um, why?"

"Because I'm only... well, I'm only *intimate* with guys I'm in a relationship with. I don't just jump into bed with people. I like to take things slow."

"Oh."

I chuckled, a bit embarrassed. "And I'd like to get to know you better," I told him. "Is that okay?"

His long fingers played with my hand, my fingers, my thumb. "Um, sure. I guess."

"If I come around tomorrow?" I hedged, still unsure. "We can just hang out, if you want. We don't have to *do* anything."

His fingers stilled on mine. "I want to," he said softly. "I want to do stuff," he admitted, as a deep blush tinted his cheeks.

I smiled, but I wanted to see his whole face. I wanted to see him. I shuffled closer, put one hand on his leg and the other held his hand.

"Isaac, can I ask something?"

He nodded.

"Can you take your glasses off?" I asked gently. "I want to see you."

He froze, but I squeezed his hand and gave him time. Eventually he said, "I don't take them off very often in front of other people."

I thought for a second he was going to say no. But then he pulled his hand from mine and slowly lifted it to his face. He took off his glasses, but kept his face down; his eyes were closed. After giving him a second, I lifted his face slowly and kissed his cheek.

And then he opened his eyes.

I had to stop myself from gasping. Oh, my God. I'd never seen eyes like his. He was waiting for some kind of response, and I had to swallow so I could speak.

Even then my voice was just a whisper, "Your eyes are so blue!"

He shrugged. "They're useless."

I took his face in my hands, to stop him from facing downward. "They're beautiful."

His eyes looked normal, apart from the striking blue color, but they looked... well, normal. They didn't look in different directions, or weren't deformed in any way. I don't know why I was expecting them to be, but they weren't. They were normal. They were beautiful.

"Isaac," I said softly. "They're not useless, they're a part of you. They make you, you." I knew showing me this was a huge show of trust from him. I kissed his face, his cheeks, his lips. "Thank you."

He gave me a small but honest smile, but he was quick to put his glasses back on. "So, about tomorrow?"

"Tomorrow," I said with a smile and another squeeze of his hand. "Tomorrow, I can be here mid-morning? And we can just take it from there."

Isaac smiled. "Sounds good."

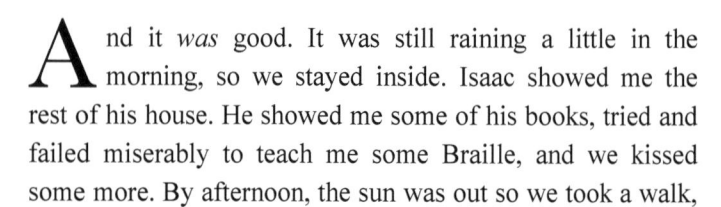

~

And it *was* good. It was still raining a little in the morning, so we stayed inside. Isaac showed me the rest of his house. He showed me some of his books, tried and failed miserably to teach me some Braille, and we kissed some more. By afternoon, the sun was out so we took a walk, not to the park but around the neighborhood.

Time just flew when I was with him. And by mid-afternoon—lunch eaten, dogs walked—we ended up back on his couch, making out. I tried not to get carried away. I knew this was new to him, but when he pulled me against him, and when he tasted my tongue with his own and moaned softly, I almost lost it.

I tried not to get carried away, letting him set the pace.

I just didn't expect him to want to move so fast. Yes, he was new to this, but he was a very quick learner. It was me who had to slow things down, as much as my body protested.

On Tuesday after work when I visited, we ended up making out, and on Thursday when I arrived for Brady's scheduled appointment, we ended up making out again. Only each time, it was a little more, a little further. He'd kiss a little deeper, a little harder, his hands would hold a little tighter, explore a little further.

Now I wasn't opposed to this, not at all, but all these little advances, left me a whole lot of aching.

And he knew it. He could feel it, how hard I was, and I could feel how hard he was. But he wasn't ready for that. And as much as it killed me, I didn't push him. But, my God, he was so responsive.

Every touch, every kiss, he reacted. Not because it was new to him, I realized, but because his senses were so heightened. If I touched him, he'd get goose bumps. If I whispered sweet nothings against his ear, he'd shiver. If I lay over him, pressing him into the sofa as I kissed him, his whole body melted.

It had only been a few weeks and it was far too soon. Maybe not for other people, maybe not for other men, but for Isaac, for us, it was. I needed to rein it in. I pulled back from him, tracing my fingers along his face, and pecked his lips once, twice.

"I should get going."

His eyes were closed, his glasses were on the coffee table, his hands still held on to me and he sighed.

"Hey," I said lightly. "I need to get home to Missy."

He nodded, but I could tell he wasn't happy.

I sat up, and pulled him up to a sitting position with me. "And to be honest, Isaac, you're killing me," I told him with a laugh.

"Oh," he mumbled. "I'm sorry."

"Don't be," I told him. "Don't ever be. Isaac, you're incredibly sexy and smart, and I really like you."

"So why are you leaving?"

"You're not ready," I told him. "I want to stay. God, I want to. God, the way you kiss me…" I took a deep breath. "But you're not ready, and Isaac, I don't want to rush you. I don't want to pressure you and I don't want to ruin this."

He smiled, sort of. "So, um, this weekend…?"

"We could go out?" I suggested. "Lunch or dinner?"

"Really?"

"Yes, really," I told him.

"Like a… like a date?"

I laughed. "I thought we were past the first date."

He smiled and ducked his head. It was adorable. I took his hand and pulled him to his feet. "Come on, you can walk me out and kiss me at the door like a proper gentleman."

There wasn't much proper-gentleman-like about the way he kissed me, that was for sure. He kissed me up against the door until my head spun. I collected Missy in a daze, and by the time I got home, I was barely through my front door before I was stripping off, seeking some relief in the shower.

∼

I met Hannah's husband, Carlos, on the Saturday when I went to Isaac's for lunch. He was a nice guy; tall, quiet and smiled adoringly at his wife every time she laughed. And having lunch with them was funny. Hannah's sense of humor, her stories, her jokes and even her facial expressions had me smiling the entire time, too. I saw so much of Isaac in her, and vice versa. He was much more serious than her, though I'd seen brief snippets of his sense of humor.

Hannah was obviously pleased with me spending time with Isaac. She tried using the two notepads tactic to write me notes, but of course, Isaac knew.

She was making a list on one, of things she needed to get for the coming week, and on the other, she wrote, *Is he treating you okay?*

As inconspicuously as I could, I gave her a nod. Then she added, *Don't let him be an ass.*

Isaac put his glass down. "Oh Hannah, give up on writing notes and just say it out loud."

She looked at me with her mouth open while Carlos and I laughed. "Yeah, he knows about the note writing apparently," I told her.

Isaac sighed. "I'm blind, not stupid."

"Jeez," Hannah griped. "I can't even talk about you behind your back anymore."

I laughed, and Isaac smiled smugly. He sipped his drink. "So, what did the note say?"

Hannah huffed. "I told Carter not to let you get away with being an ass," she said flatly. "But oops, too late."

I laughed, and Isaac turned his face toward me. "Something funny?"

"Yep, absolutely," I said, knowing he'd hear the smile in my voice. "You two are funny."

Hannah slid her arm around Carlos' waist and grinned. Then she said, "So what are you two doing this afternoon?"

"I thought we might go for a walk," I told them. "Then go out for dinner."

Her face lit up. "Where to?"

"I don't know," I admitted. "Isaac, you feel like Italian, Thai, Chinese, burgers?"

"Um," he smiled thoughtfully, "Italian."

I looked at Hannah and Carlos. "Italian it is."

She smiled at me warmly, then turned to her brother. "Well, we'll be off, leave you boys to it." Then she looked back at me. "And remember, don't let him get away with being an ass." She kissed Isaac on the cheek, and gave me another smile.

Carlos shook my hand. "Nice to finally meet you," he said, and they walked out.

When they were gone, I said, "Carlos is a nice guy."

"He is," Isaac agreed, then gently pushed his dirty plate from in front of him. "I'm sorry about Hannah though," he said. "She has no filter. She called me an ass."

I smiled, leaned over and kissed his cheek. "Don't apologize. I happen to really like ass."

Isaac's mouth fell open, as he blushed a deep scarlet, and I laughed. "Come on, on your feet. I'll wash, you dry."

He shook his head, disbelievingly. "I can't believe you just said that!"

"What?" I scoffed. "That you're drying the dishes? Fair's fair, Isaac."

He blushed again and bit his lip. "That's not what I'm talking about, and you know it."

I put the dishes in the sink, laughing. "Yeah, I know. Next time, I'll ask Hannah to call you a dick, because I happen to really like that too."

Isaac laughed. "Carter!"

I pulled his chin between my thumb and forefinger, and with smiling lips, I kissed him. "Was that too crass for you?"

He smiled. "No, I guess not. Just unexpected," he said, and when I tried to step back toward the sink, his hand on my arm stopped me. "Carter…"

"What is it, Isaac?"

"Um, I've been thinking, and I know you said you thought I wasn't ready for anything too physical…"

His words died away. I could tell he was embarrassed, so I leaned right up against him and spoke soft near his ear. "Yes."

He swallowed hard. "Well, I think I am."

"Ready for what?"

"More."

I pulled back to look at his face. "Isaac, are you telling me you want to—"

"Not sex," he said quickly. "But other stuff…"

I bit back a groan. Fuck. My willpower around him was waning fast. "Isaac…"

"I'm not going to beg," he said gruffly. Then his hands settled on my hips and he pulled me against his. "But I know you want to. I can feel it."

Oh, fuck.

"I'd never make you beg," I murmured before I kissed him. Hard.

My hands were on his face, in his hair, down his back, over his ass. I pushed him gently against the countertop, pressing against him, never breaking the kiss.

He was hard.

And I couldn't stop myself. I reached between us and palmed his dick through the denim of his jeans. He groaned in my mouth and bucked his hips into my hand. He needed more.

So did I.

With fumbling hands, I unbuttoned his jeans and slid my hand under the waistband of his briefs, skin on skin, and wrapped my fingers around him.

He froze. Then he shuddered and moaned.

I kissed him harder, plunging my tongue into his mouth. I squeezed my hand around him, and pumped him as best I could. He whimpered and his body jerked against me, flexing hard and with a guttural groan, he came.

His head fell back and he shot hot and thick over his shirt and my hand, until he slumped forward, shaking and falling into me.

"Jesus, Isaac, are you okay?"

"Mm, very okay," he mumbled into my neck.

I wrapped my other hand around his neck and held him against me. "Shit, Isaac, I wanted your first time to be something special."

He chuckled. "That was something special."

I laughed. "You know what I mean." I pulled back from him and looked down at the mess. "Come on, you need to get cleaned up." I took him by the hand and led us back through the living room to the foyer and headed for the bedrooms. "Which room is yours?"

"Last door at the end of the hall," he told me.

His room was huge, like the rest of the house. The large bed had a dark wood frame that was decked in gold and navy covers along with pillows. There were two doors along one wall. I could see an en-suite bathroom through one, so, still holding his hand, I walked us in there.

"If you tell me where to find the washcloths, I'll go grab one while you strip down," I suggested. "Or did you just want to have a shower?"

He hesitated for a second. "If I were to have a shower," he cleared his throat, "would you join me?"

Jesus.

"Um..."

"It'd be only fair," he said lightly.

"Fair?"

"That I return the favor."

Oh, God. "Isaac, I don't expect—"

"I want you to."

I reached up and softly touched his face, then leaned up and softly kissed his lips. Then I took off his glasses, and told him, "I like the water hot."

He smiled. "Good, so do I."

I helped him out of his cum-stained shirt and watched as he pushed his jeans down, leaving his still semi-hard cock hanging long and heavy. It made my mouth water.

"Oh, God," I mumbled, then remembered I was supposed to be getting undressed. I frantically pulled my shirt over my head, toed my shoes off and when I undid my jeans, I almost groaned in relief.

I was so hard, and he was so beautiful. He was lean and toned, pale skin with trails of dark hair in all the right places. As he leaned into the shower and turned the water on, I watched his muscles slide under his skin, how his ribs and abs stretched.

Then he stepped in under the water, and it was worse. Or better. Because he was even hotter wet. The way the water ran over him, washing him clean. Jesus, this was going to be over embarrassingly quick.

"Carter?"

"Yeah," I answered. "Just admiring the view."

His head tilted to one side, not too sure what I meant.

"You, Isaac," I told him as I walked into the shower. "Just admiring you."

"Oh."

As soon as I stepped in next to him, it was different. This wasn't a spontaneous, frantic, had-to-have hand job in the kitchen. This was calculated and intentional. I was suddenly nervous.

And so was he. "I've never done this before."

I ran my hands over his chest, up his neck and held his face. I kissed him soft and slow, in the steaming hot water. I kissed down his jaw, up to his ear. "Just do what feels right."

Then his hands were on me, my sides, my waist, my stomach, but he seemed to hesitate in going any lower. I slid my hand over his, and asked him, "Are you sure?"

He nodded and whispered, "Yes."

So with my fingers over his, I slid our hands down and wrapped his hand around my cock, making us both gasp.

"Oh, my God," he murmured, his wet lips moved against my skin as his hand worked me over. "You feel so hot. You're so hard." He pumped me, sliding, squeezing.

His touch, his lips, his hand, his words, and I was done. "Fuck," I groaned, as pleasure ripped through me, pulsing onto Isaac in thick bursts. My hands were out to the sides, on the tiled walls, and he squeezed and pumped me while the entire room spun.

Pressing me against the wall of the shower, Isaac kissed my neck and my shoulder, until the orgasm fog cleared from my brain. But even in the haze of my mind, I could feel him hard again, pressed hot against me.

So this time, as I caught my breath, I went slow. I soaped him up, and washed him down, taking in every inch of his body. There was no urgency, not like the first time in the kitchen. I took my time, let him feel every bit of it, savor it. I kissed and nipped at his neck, his jaw, his ears. He was wantonly thrusting his cock into my fist, moaning when I cupped his balls and drew his orgasm out for as long as he could stand.

When he could take no more, his whole body trembled and he cried out as he came. It was beautiful to watch.

I turned off the water, and dried Isaac off with a towel. He was thoroughly and deliciously spent. So I quickly dried myself and leaned up and kissed him. "How was that? Do you feel okay?"

Isaac gave me a blissed out, lazy smile. "I feel great."

I laughed. "How about we get dressed and veg out on the sofa for a bit?"

"Sounds good."

"And Isaac?"

"Yeah?"

"Just so you know, I don't normally cum that quick, but I was so turned on already, and then the way you spoke to me…"

His face tilted toward me. "Was that wrong?"

"Oh, no," I said with a laugh. "It was very right."

He gave me a smug smile.

"And Isaac?"

"Yeah?"

I kissed him softly. "For what it's worth, I'm glad you were ready."

~

Dinner was interesting. There was a little Italian café not too far from Isaac's place that he knew, and I figured sticking with somewhere he was at least familiar with would be ideal.

The staff were great, didn't bat an eyelid at Brady, and no one seemed to care that two guys were dining together. I read the daily specials to him, we ordered, and started to talk.

I'd never been on a date with a blind person before, but it was really no different than any other date. Except for the guide dog curled up at our feet. I did make a point of requesting no broccoli, to which Isaac smiled, and I did tell him the waiter put his glass of water at eleven o'clock, but that was it.

We simply spent the night eating good food, and talking. I asked questions that had bothered me over the last few weeks, but I'd never been game enough to ask.

"Such as?" Isaac asked warily.

"Well, your phone?" I started. "It's a touch screen. How do you know what to press? I've seen you talking on your phone, but never dialing someone. And I've seen a laptop with your work stuff. How do you know what you're typing or reading if it's not in Braille?"

Isaac smiled at my slew of questions. "iPhones have synthetic speech. All my commands, messages, numbers are all voice activated. My laptop has a screen-reader. It can read any text, letter, email and my keyboard has a Braille cover. We have a Braille labeler for things around the house."

I remembered how the dictionary had a Braille label. "Wow. That's pretty amazing."

Isaac smiled. "Well, technology sure has made it easier. The difference from when I was at school, to what I teach now is phenomenal."

"I could just imagine," I said, though the truth was, I could barely imagine it at all. I couldn't begin to imagine what it would be like to have my eyesight taken away from me.

Before our conversation took a depressing turn, I changed the subject. "Oh, next weekend," I started. "What are you doing?"

Isaac put down his fork. "Um, I'm not sure," he hedged. "Why?"

"Well, Mark is visiting, and he wants to meet you," I reminded him. "And I'd like you to meet him."

"Oh." He was clearly surprised. "Um…"

"I promise he'll be on his best behavior," I told him. "He gets here on Friday night and leaves on Sunday at lunchtime, so he'll take up all of my weekend. If you say you'll meet him, then at least I get to spend a little bit of time with you."

"So if I don't meet him, I don't spend any time with you all weekend?" he asked, his lips twisting in a smug pout. "Did you just try to blackmail me?"

I chuckled. "I did. Did it work?"

He smiled. "Maybe."

I smiled. "We can come around on Saturday, if that's okay with you?"

He tried not to smile. "Maybe."

"Are you trying to play hard to get?"

He grinned. "Maybe."

I laughed. "Well, it won't work. After this afternoon, in your kitchen and shower, I know you're not."

He chuckled. "Yeah, about that," he said, shifting in his seat. He bit his lip. "I thought that was something we could work on again tonight."

I looked around the café for the waiter. I put my hand up to get his attention. "Check, please."

Isaac laughed.

## 8

Mark got to my place late on Friday, and we spent the night sprawled out on my sofas— he on one, me on the other—drinking beer and talking shit.

We traded stories of our jobs, what was new, how things were for both of us. He told me all the gossip of Hartford, how it was still the same people, same boring shit, different day. I told him about the animal hospital, the people I worked with, the animals I'd met.

Then, of course, he asked me about Isaac.

I smiled when I thought about him—when I talked about him. I couldn't help it. I told Mark how I'd seen him twice during the week, after work on Tuesday and Thursday, staying until nearly midnight both times.

"So," Mark said, grinning. "Things have been moving along in the bedroom then?"

I rolled my eyes, but grinned. Yes, they had. I gave Isaac his first ever blow job on Tuesday night, and his second on Thursday night, in which he *gave* his first blow job in return. I looked at Mark, still grinning. "I'm not telling you anything!"

Mark looked at me, shocked, then shook his head at me. "Oh, my God. You really like this guy."

I smiled. There wasn't any point in denying it. "Yeah, I do." Then I pointed my beer bottle at him. "And you'd better be on your best behavior tomorrow. No rude jokes, no lewd comments, and *no* blind jokes."

Mark laughed.

I reminded him again in the Jeep on our way over to Isaac's house on Saturday. "Please be nice to him," I said as we pulled into the drive. "I don't want you fucking things up for me with him by being an ass."

He silently crossed his heart, but then he laughed. I gave him the stink-eye, and let Missy out of the Jeep. She ran ahead, sniffing her way to the front door, and we followed.

I pressed the doorbell, nudged Mark with my elbow, and whispered, "Be nice."

Isaac opened the door, looking his usual gorgeous self. He was dressed in cargos and an expensive polo shirt, his leather loafers, and his trademark sunglasses.

He smiled. "Hey."

"Hi," I replied, kissing his cheek, stepping in next to him, and taking his left hand.

Mark was smiling hugely, and Isaac held out his hand. "You must be Mark?"

Mark quickly took Isaac's hand, shaking it firmly. "Yep, that's me. You're the Isaac I keep hearing about?"

Isaac smiled. "I guess that's me." He stepped aside, inviting Mark in and closed the door behind him. "Come on in."

Isaac and I walked in first, with me still holding his hand. I knew he was nervous, and I wanted to reassure him. Mark followed us in to the kitchen and leaned against the counter next to me.

"So," Isaac said. "Can I get anyone a drink?"

"Sure," I answered.

Isaac dropped my hand and, when he opened the fridge door, he asked, "Mark? Would you like something to drink?"

"Ah yeah, okay. Thanks," Mark said. Then looked at me and mouthed the words "He doesn't look blind."

Isaac stopped and turned to face us. "Something wrong?"

I smiled. His intuition was amazing. Mark looked a little amazed at how Isaac knew we were talking about him, and then he stupidly waved his hand in the air, as if trying to catch Isaac out.

Mark was a lot of things. I never said he was bright.

I shook my head and laughed at him. "No, nothing's wrong, Isaac. Mark here is making rude hand gestures to see if you're really blind."

Isaac turned to the sound of my voice. "What is he? Twelve?"

"Sometimes."

"Hey!" Mark defended himself. "I'm right here!"

I laughed, and Isaac smiled as he took the large jug of iced tea from the fridge.

"And it wasn't *rude* hand gestures," Mark said petulantly. "It was more of a… waving…"

Isaac snorted. "That sounded a lot more intelligent in your head, didn't it?"

I laughed, and Mark nodded. "Well, yeah. It did."

Then Isaac poured three glasses of iced tea, and Mark watched him; how his long fingers felt the edge of the glass, how he moved the jug, how he felt the spout against the glass, how he poured three drinks, of equal measure, without spilling a drop. I couldn't help but smile a little proudly.

Isaac asked, "Did Missy go straight out the back?"

"Yeah, she went to find Brady, I presume."

Isaac nodded. "Do you want to go out in the backyard?" he asked. "We can sit out there if you'd prefer."

I touched his arm. "Sounds great."

So we sat at the outside patio table, enjoying the beautiful summer day while the dogs sniffed and explored.

Once we'd sat down, the conversation started with Isaac asking Mark, "Apart from waving at blind men, what do you do?"

Mark laughed, and the banter between them began. Isaac was relaxed, in his element even, and I realized maybe the initial nervousness wasn't Isaac's at all. It was mine. I wanted them to get along. I wanted them to like each other.

Mark was his usual charming, amusing self and the three of us chatted easily for the better part of an hour. When Isaac offered to get us bottled water, he was barely to the back door when Mark tried to whisper, "I can see why you like him. He's fucking hot!"

I smiled at Mark. "And he has really good hearing."

Mark's smile died and one eyebrow lifted. "Did he just hear me say that?"

"I'm blind," Isaac called out from inside. "Not deaf."

I laughed, and Mark whacked my arm and hissed at me, "You could have told me!" Then his smile softened, and he said quietly, "He's a real nice guy, Carter."

I looked at Mark and gave him a nod and a smile. "I know."

We spent the afternoon at the park, and I thought maybe seeing Isaac with his guide dog would freak Mark out a little —or make it more real somehow—but it didn't. He was just cool with it. While we sat on the bench seat, Brady stayed at Isaac's feet, Mark threw a ball for Missy, and when he grew tired of that, he put Missy on her lead and told us he'd try using her as a "chick-or-dick" magnet for unsuspecting parkgoers.

I cringed inside. "I'm sorry," I apologized to Isaac. "He has no filter, and no shame."

Isaac chuckled. "Chick or dick magnet?"

"Yeah, he's not fussy," I explained. "If it has a pulse, or looks remotely human, he's interested."

Mark grinned. "Some didn't even have that going for them," he said with a laugh. Then he amended, "Well, they had a pulse."

"Behave," I warned him.

Mark just laughed as he walked off with my dog, and Isaac chuckled beside me. "He's funny."

"He's crazy," I told him. "I should have him tested."

Isaac laughed, then he reached out his hand, as if looking for mine. I put my hand in his and he gave mine a squeeze. "Thank you, for today. It's been great."

I rubbed my thumb over the back of his hand. "You're very welcome."

Isaac smiled and was quiet for a short while. "Is he really bi-sexual?"

"Yep. He sure is. Why do you ask?"

Isaac shrugged. "I thought I was for a while, you know, not gay." He shook his head. "When I was younger, I had a friend… who was a girl, and I thought I liked her *that way*. I guess I did like her that way. But then I met Daniel, and I *knew* I liked him, but I thought it was normal to like girls, not boys, so I kissed her."

"And?"

"And nothing. Absolutely nothing. I mean, it was sweet and exciting…" he sighed. "And so I thought I must be bi. I thought I must just be wired to like both boys and girls. I had no intention of being with a guy, you know, being blind was hard enough. But when I was in study class with Daniel, and he kissed me?" He smiled and shook his head. "It was like a light bulb over my head."

I smiled and squeezed his hand. "And you realized you didn't like girls as much as you thought you did?"

Isaac chuckled and nodded. "Something like that."

"It wasn't too different for me," I admitted. "I was a late bloomer, I guess. Not much happened for me until I went to college. But I pretty much knew right through high school that I liked guys, I just didn't act on it until later." Then I thought about it, how much harder it would have been for Isaac not being able to see guys, or girls, to see which he was more attracted to. "How did you know you liked guys if you couldn't check them out?"

Isaac chuckled. "Same as you. You just know you like guys," he said. "By the sound of a guy's voice, how he smells."

"Smells?" I asked incredulously. "As in body odor?"

He grinned. "Or lack of. His deodorant, his cologne." Then Isaac blushed a little. "Like yours."

"Mine?"

He smiled and gave a shy nod. "You smell very nice."

"Oh."

He looked a little smug. "And there's always porn."

I sputtered. "Porn?"

Isaac laughed and nodded. "God, I remember telling Hannah I wasn't sure if I liked girls or boys, and she asked me to visualize what kind of porn I wanted to listen to late at night. She asked if I pictured a man and woman, or two men?" He sighed. "And I had my answer."

"You pictured two men?"

"Every time."

I laughed. Then I thought about it. "You *listen* to porn?"

Isaac ducked his head and chuckled. "There are some very vocal videos."

I groaned at the sudden ache in my groin. "I'm all for discussing this further, and even trying it, but right now we need to change the topic, or I'll be walking home funny."

Isaac threw his head back and laughed, just as Mark came back. He smiled at the sight of Isaac laughing, sat down beside us, and sighed.

"No luck?" I asked.

"Nah, Missy's lost her mojo."

I snorted. "Yeah, it's the dog's fault."

Mark leaned forward and gave Missy a rub and a pat, and she wagged her tail in kind. Mark looked at Brady, who still lay at Isaac's feet, and I knew he saw that Isaac didn't show the dog an ounce of affection. My friend looked from the guide dog to me, and I gave him a small smile and shrug.

"So," Isaac said, interrupting our silent exchange. "What are you two doing tonight?"

Mark stretched his feet out in front of him and his hands over his head and yawned. "Dinner then clubbing. If I can't pick up in the park with a dog, then I'll just have to show them how I dance."

I laughed. "Great. A pity fuck."

Isaac's mouth fell open, and Mark laughed. "Hey, whatever it takes." Then he looked at Isaac and told him, "Isaac, you should come with us!"

"Oh, I don't think so." Isaac shook his head. "Thanks anyway."

Mark asked, "Have you ever been to a nightclub?"

Isaac answered quietly. "No. Not the safest place for me, I'd imagine."

I squeezed his hand. "If you want to come with us, I promise I'll take care of you. I won't drink, and I won't take my hand off you, you'll know you're safe the entire time." I rather liked the idea of dancing with him.

Isaac turned to face me. "I won't, but thank you for asking."

"That's okay, I'll probably be busy babysitting Mark anyway," I said with a shrug. Then I leaned in and whispered in Isaac's ear, "We can always slow dance at your place anyway."

Isaac cleared his throat and smiled. He leaned into me, and whispered back, "Now that sounds good."

"All right, you two," Mark declared. "Enough of the lovey-dovey shit. We're definitely going to a gay bar tonight. If I'm gonna watch two guys fawn over each other, it may as well be where I can get some."

Isaac laughed. "Does he always talk like that?"

I nodded. "Always."

Walking back to Isaac's place, he kept his hand on my arm. Again, not really needing the guidance, but just to touch me. It was almost like we were holding hands. Almost. And when it came time to say goodbye, Mark took Missy and harnessed her into the backseat, giving me and Isaac some privacy.

We stood just inside his front door. "Have fun tonight," he said quietly.

I leaned into him and slid one hand along his jaw. "Can I come over on Tuesday after work?" He nodded, and I pressed my lips to his. His hands slid around my back, he opened his mouth for me and kissed me deeply. I melted into him, his touch, his taste, and as his tongue slid into my mouth, my cock stirred.

With a reluctant groan, I slowed the kiss and pulled my lips from his. I rested my forehead on his cheek, trying to catch my breath. "God, Isaac..." I murmured, to him or to myself, I wasn't sure. I took a small step back, but cupped his face in my hands. "I meant what I said about the slow dancing."

I left him smiling in the doorway.

We'd barely made it a block from Isaac's when Mark said, "He's a great guy, Carter…"

"But?"

"But what's the deal with his dog?" Mark shrugged. "I don't get it, Brady's a beautiful dog. Smarter than Missy here, and that's saying something. So why doesn't he touch him?"

I knew this was coming. I'd seen the look he gave me in the park when he was patting Missy. I sighed. "I'm not sure."

"But you've noticed it?" Mark clarified. "The way he ignores him, doesn't pat him, doesn't even acknowledge him? I mean, I met the guy for a few hours and even I could see that."

"Of course I noticed."

"But you haven't asked him?"

"Well, no," I hedged. "What can I say? It's not illegal to *not* pat your dog. I figure he'll open up to me when he's ready. I don't want to push him."

"Because you're falling for him," Mark said, like he was stating the obvious.

"What?"

"Oh, come on," Mark said. "Blindness isn't contagious, is it? Surely you can see that."

I rolled my eyes at him, but pretended to concentrate on driving. Was I? Was I falling in love with Isaac? I mean, I loved spending time with him, I loved talking with him, hearing his point of view on the world, I loved how he kissed me, how he touched me, I loved…

Oh, fuck.

Mark snorted. "For a guy who graduated college with a four-point-oh average, you're pretty fucking stupid."

Mark didn't say much more on the matter, well, not until he'd had one too many drinks later that night. We were on the crowded, thumping dance floor and he could tell I was still distracted. He spun me around full circle, pulled me in close and whisper-shouted in my ear, "He won't hurt you. He's not like Paul. He won't cheat on you and break your heart."

He let me go with a laugh, turned and found some random stranger to grind against. I left the dance floor, found a seat and watched Mark dance. I shook my head and smiled at him when ten minutes later, he grinned at me as they disappeared into the bathroom.

I knew Isaac wouldn't hurt me. Not the way Paul had. I wouldn't walk in one day and find Isaac in bed with another guy. He just simply wasn't the type. But that didn't mean he still couldn't hurt me, or break my heart.

# 9

I wasn't joking when I told Isaac I wanted to dance with him, and when I arrived at his place after work on Tuesday, I didn't waste a minute.

It was all I'd thought about.

So when I walked through the door, I pulled him in for a quick kiss. "Is Hannah still here?"

"No," Isaac replied warily. "She left about an hour ago."

"Good," I said, pulling him into the living room. "I've wanted to do this for three days."

"Do what?" Isaac asked. I could tell he was worried, but he was smiling.

"Dance."

"What?"

I laughed. "Do you have a dock for your iPhone?"

He turned his face toward the far wall cabinet, and I could see the dock. "Um, yes?"

I smiled. "Well, we'll need music."

He scratched his head. "Um..."

"Stay here," I told him. I walked over, pulled out my iPhone, scrolled through my playlists, and plugged it in. I

*Blind Faith*

pressed play, turned the volume up and walked back over to him.

"This really isn't my kind of music," he told me.

I slid my hand around his waist and pulled him against me. "The music doesn't matter." I held his hips against mine, and we started to sway. "Can you feel the beat?"

He nodded.

"The thump, thump, thump in your chest?"

He nodded again, his hands wound around my back and I could feel him give in. He started to move with me.

I skimmed my hands over his hips, up his waist, over his body. "Can you feel it?"

He whispered, "Yes."

Isaac moved pretty well for someone who'd never danced. He swayed against me, keeping his hips aligned with mine. I could feel his reaction to me, how hard he was, how much he wanted me. So I raked my hands over his ass and pulled him against me, rubbing our cocks together through our clothes.

I trailed my lips over the skin of his neck. "I've wanted to do this since Saturday," I told him, kissing his neck, up to his jaw. His hands found my face and he pulled my mouth to his, kissing me so fucking hard.

He was pushing me back toward the sofa, but I stopped him. "Bedroom?"

We'd ended up in his room before, the first time I'd had him in my mouth, and when he tasted me, only this time we would have each other. We fell onto his bed, kissing, holding, licking and touching and by the time we were both naked, I showed him what I wanted to do.

He was lying down, his head near the pillows, his long cock was hard and waiting. So I kissed down his body, over his chest, his stomach, and licked him from base to tip. He groaned, but as I settled down next to him, my hips near his face and rolled us on our sides, he understood what I wanted him to do.

He learned every inch of my body, mapping me with his fingers and his mouth. He was new to the art of fellatio, but my God, he was learning.

I wrapped my arms around his hips and sucked him as deep as I could. Isaac's whole body went rigid, flexing hard, and his cock surged in my mouth and with a strangled cry he came down my throat.

His whole body shook and shuddered as his orgasm subsided, and when I tried to pull away from him, his arms wrapped tighter around me. His nose nuzzled into my pubic hair and he inhaled.

"It's your turn."

He took his time with me, licking, sucking, learning. His fingers were everywhere, pulling my balls, rubbing over my hole. And when I warned him I was about to cum, he didn't pull away. He pumped my shaft and sucked harder on the head, and I came in his mouth.

He grunted, then he gagged.

Even as my head spun, and my insides were warm Jell-O, I could see he shuddered as he swallowed. He sat up and grimaced. "That wasn't particularly pleasant," he said.

I laughed, and I pulled him down so he was laying the same way as me. I pulled him against me, tucking him into my side. "Oh, baby, I tried to warn you."

"I wanted to taste it," he said quietly.

I tilted his face up to mine and kissed him, sweeping my tongue into his mouth. "Does my mouth taste better?"

"Hmm," he hummed. "Much."

I rolled us over, so I was completely on top of him, both of us completely naked. "You just need to practice."

His fingers traced the sides of my face. "You don't mind?"

*Blind Faith*

I laughed. "It'd be my pleasure."

And for the next three or four weeks, that's exactly what it was. Well, my pleasure, his pleasure, we weren't keeping count.

We spent as much time together as we could, usually ending up in his bedroom. Or on the sofa. Or in the shower. I'd told him about the tattoo on my left hip, and as though he could see it, he never failed to touch it, kiss it, lick it. We still hadn't had intercourse sex, but just about everything else. Though it wasn't *all* physical.

We talked about most things, though he was still yet to open up to me about his parents or the accident, which left him blind. He didn't *have* to tell me. I just wondered if he would.

I wondered what I'd have to do, what would have to happen, to make him tell me.

∼

It was Sunday, after Isaac and I had been together almost two months, when my cell phone rang. It was work. I frowned at my phone, but took the call. "Carter Reece speaking."

"Carter, it's Kate from the animal hospital. I'm sorry to bother you on a Sunday."

"Kate, it's fine," I told her. "What's wrong?"

"I've just had a call from old Mrs Yeo," she said softly. "Her cat, Mr Whiskers, passed away."

Oh, hell.

"She's very upset."

"I'll go see her," I told her. "I'm on my way."

I clicked off the call, and Isaac was beside me. "Carter, what's wrong?"

"Mrs Yeo, the little old lady who's on my house call list," I said softly. "I stop in to see her before you on Thursdays. Well, her old cat Mr Whiskers passed away. She's very upset."

Isaac squeezed my hand. "You should go."

"Yes, I should." Then I stopped and looked at him. "Can I leave Missy here? Is that okay?"

"Sure, of course," he said quickly. But as I got to the door, Isaac called out, "Carter?"

I stopped. "Yeah?"

"I could come with you."

"Ah," I hesitated. "Are you sure?"

He stood up. "If it's okay. She might need someone to sit with her while you... look after Mr Whiskers."

"Okay," I agreed.

He grabbed his house keys and walked toward me. He clearly had no intention of bringing Brady.

"What about Brady?"

"He can stay here with Missy. They can use the dog-door to the backyard, they'll be fine."

I smiled. "I know they'll be okay. What about you?"

He stopped and I could see a slight flinch in his shoulders. "You'll be with me, won't you?"

"Of course," I said quickly. "Of course I will be."

"Then I'll be fine."

When I pulled the Jeep in front of Mrs Yeo's little house, I hurried around to Isaac's side. He put his hand on my arm, and we walked up the two steps and knocked on the front door. When Mrs Yeo opened the door, the tiny woman's eyes welled with tears.

"Mrs Yeo, I came as soon as I heard."

"Please come in," she said, and as soon as we'd walked into her living room, she asked, "Who is this?"

"Mrs Yeo, this is Isaac Brannigan. He's… my boyfriend. I was with him when Kate phoned me."

"Oh," she said quietly. She looked at how Isaac's hand was on my forearm, then to his sunglasses. "Is he blind?"

"Yes, I am," Isaac told her.

"Oh," she said with a nod. "My doctor says I have only half sight in my left eye."

"That's no good, Mrs Yeo," Isaac said gently.

"Please, sit down," she said, waving her hand at the old orange and brown floral sofa. "Can I get you boys a drink?"

I led Isaac in front of the sofa and sat down with him. "Don't worry about us, Mrs Yeo, we're fine," I told her, not wanting her to fuss. But I needed to ask the dreaded question. "Tell me, Mrs Yeo, what happened with Mr Whiskers?"

She sighed sadly. "He's been off his food these last two days, and I worry," she said in her broken English. "And this morning I couldn't find him. He'd never go far. He's too old. But he wasn't asleep on his chair," she said with a pointed glance to the old brown rocking chair by the front window.

Then she looked at me, and her bottom lip trembled. "I found him in the back garden."

It was typical of cats to go away from home to die. I nodded, and asked her softly, "Where is he now?"

"I put him in a box," she said, dabbing at her eyes with a crumpled handkerchief. "On the garden table."

I nodded, and Isaac slipped his hand from my forearm into my hand. I gave his hand a gentle squeeze. "Mrs Yeo, can I ask what you'd like to do with Mr Whiskers?"

She dabbed at her eyes with her handkerchief. "I like to bury him, here in the garden, I think."

"Mrs Yeo, would you like me to help bury him?" I asked. "I can dig the hole for you and we can stay while you say goodbye."

She nodded and started to cry. "Would you be so kind?"

Isaac answered, his voice was rough. "Of course we can."

Mrs Yeo told me there was a garden shovel by the back door, just through the kitchen.

I told Isaac I wouldn't be long, and as I walked out, I heard Mrs Yeo ask him, the only way a ninety-something year old woman could, "So how were you blinded?"

It was something I'd wanted to talk about with him for two months, but never had the courage to ask, and little Mrs Yeo, who had met him only minutes ago, just asked him point blank.

"It was a car accident," Isaac told her. "I was eight years old."

As much as I wanted to listen, I knew I shouldn't, and I knew as soon as Isaac heard the back door shut, he'd know I'd heard what he told her already.

So I busied myself digging a hole in the garden, trying not to think about what he was telling a complete stranger and wouldn't tell me. It was a warm fall afternoon and digging the hole was hard going. I could tell the garden would have once been beautiful, but it was too big for Mrs Yeo on her own. The flowers were finished for the year; the leaves were falling from the trees, making an untidy mess on the un-mowed lawn.

When I was done, I walked back inside to hear Mrs Yeo talk about a friend of an old neighbor who had a guide dog, and I wondered if the course of that conversation had included Brady, or even Rosie, the guide dog Isaac had before Brady, the one whose death broke his heart.

I wanted to have that conversation with him. I wanted him to open up to me, not to someone else. Then the realization he was here consoling a grieving elderly woman stabbed me with guilt and shame.

*Blind Faith*

Isaac turned his face toward me, obviously hearing my approach. I smiled at the sight of him, then looked to the tiny woman across from him. "Mrs Yeo? When you're ready."

I walked over to Isaac and put his hand on my arm. Following Mrs Yeo, I led Isaac out to the backyard. Mrs Yeo took Isaac's arm while I lowered the box into the makeshift grave and filled the hole back in with soil.

Mrs Yeo said some quiet words while Isaac and I stood back. When she was done, she dried her tears then hugged and thanked us both. She offered to make us some tea, but I explained we should be going. She said she'd make herself some tea anyway and retire to bed early, then she thanked us again.

"I like Dr Fields enough," she told me bluntly. "But I like you too." She patted Isaac's hand on my forearm. "I don't mind if boys love boys. If you're lucky enough to find someone to love, you hold onto them."

Changing the topic, I told her I'd keep her scheduled house call for Thursday, and she could make me a cup of that green tea. It would be a good excuse to call in and check on this tiny, frail, very-alone, heartbroken woman.

Isaac was quiet on the way back to his place. I put my hand on his knee in a show of support, but not wanting to push him, I never said a word. It wasn't until we were back at his house, that he sat on his sofa and started to talk.

"Mrs Yeo told me she had Mr Whiskers for seventeen years," he said quietly. "She got him when her husband died." I sat beside him, facing him and took his hand. "She told me losing Mr Whiskers was like losing her husband all over again."

Then he took a deep breath and squeezed my hand. "I know exactly what that's like, Carter. I know exactly how hard that is."

I knew he was about to open up to me, so I pulled him against me and cradled him in my arms while he talked.

"I don't remember the accident. I was only eight. I remember things before that of course, I remember what some things look like. I remember what my mom looked like..." His words trailed off, and I tightened my arms around him.

"But I don't remember the accident. I woke up three days later in the hospital. I knew I was awake, but my face and my eyes were bandaged so it was dark anyway. It hurt. I remember that. They told me I was in a car wreck, and that my mother didn't make it."

"Oh, baby."

He sighed. "And then when they took the bandages off and I opened my eyes, it was still dark. I was confused at first, like I couldn't get my eyes to open, even though I knew they were open." He shook his head.

He was quiet for a long moment. "Wanna know something funny?" he asked rhetorically. "I was afraid of the dark. When I was little, right up until the accident, I had to sleep with the light on."

"Oh, Isaac, baby," was the only thing I could say. All this time I'd wanted him to tell me, and now I didn't know what to say. I kissed the side of his head.

"I got my first guide dog when I was nine. His name was Cody. That's him in the photo of me when I was little," he said, waving his hand toward the mantelpiece where the photo frames were. "He helped me a lot. I don't know if I'd have been so resilient, so independent if it weren't for him.

"He was with me until I was about fourteen, and then after him, I got Rosie. Rosie was... Rosie was special. She was my best friend. We went everywhere together, school and hiking. There are photos on the mantel of me and her up on the Wompatuck State trail," he said softly. "But it was more than that. It was a hard time for me…." He cleared his throat. "My dad didn't handle losing his wife and having a blind son very well, and he drank a lot. He wasn't well…" Isaac turned in my arms to lie on his side, kind of snuggling down into me.

"It was hard. I was trying to finish school and dealing with being gay. I had Hannah, but she had her hands full with looking after Dad," he continued softly. "And I had Rosie. She was it. My rock."

He fell silent, so I kissed the top of his head again. "What happened?"

"She was going deaf," he said quietly. "She just got real old, real quick. Or so it seemed to me. At the very end, she ended up with diabetes."

I remembered Dr Fields telling me Isaac spent two years looking after his sick dog. Long ago taken out of commission, he looked after her anyway.

"You must have loved her very much."

He nodded against my chest, and whispered, "And when she died, it was like I'd lost my sight all over again."

I wanted to cry. I wanted to tell him I was sorry, but all I could do was pull him tight against me and kiss his forehead.

Mark might have thought I was in love with Isaac four weeks ago, and maybe I was. But in that moment, I knew, *I knew*, with every fiber of my being, in that very moment, I was in love with Isaac Brannigan.

## 10

We stayed on the sofa, all wrapped up in our own little world, and Isaac was so quiet, lost in his own head, that I thought he'd fallen asleep. But then he sighed. "You, um, you introduced me to Mrs Yeo as your boyfriend."

I blinked back my surprise. "I did."

"I've never been introduced as anyone's boyfriend before."

It never occurred to me he wouldn't *want* to be my boyfriend. "Is that okay?"

He tightened his arms around me. "Yes."

I grinned and kissed the top of his head. "Good, because you've been my boyfriend in my head for weeks."

He chuckled against my chest. He was quiet for a long moment, then he said, "Carter, will you stay tonight?"

Maybe he felt me freeze, maybe he heard my heart hammer in my chest, because he quickly added, "Missy's here, so you don't have to go home to her, and you can leave for work from here. Missy can even stay here tomorrow if you like…"

I smiled. "I think Missy spends more time here than she

does at my place anyway." I pulled Isaac in tight and kissed his hair again. "I'd really like that."

He sat up, suddenly nervous. "I'm not, I'm not sure if I'm ready..." he hesitated, "...you know, for sex. You've been really patient with me, and I..."

I sat up and pulled his face between my hands. "Hey, Isaac, listen. I don't expect anything, certainly not sex. What we do in the bedroom already is more than enough. You know some gay couples never have anal sex, they don't want to or they don't like it, or whatever. There's a dozen reasons—"

"I want to." He cut me off. "I want to, eventually."

"Whenever you're ready."

He smiled. "You're so good to me."

I kissed him softly. I wanted to tell him I loved him. I wanted him to know, but something stopped me. Love was something that terrified him; his reaction to Brady was evidence of that. Well, it wasn't love that scared him, it was having that love taken away from him that scared him.

So as much as I wanted to say those three words, I didn't. Instead, we ordered dinner and fell into bed. It had been an emotionally charged day, so eventually climbing into bed and holding him in my arms was perfect.

But those three little words haunted me all week. Every time I saw him, touched him, spoke to him, the words were there. In the back of my mind, on the tip of my tongue, and on Thursday when I saw him, I said them.

Isaac and I had finished dinner and were standing in the kitchen, when I told him I'd called in to see Mrs Yeo, like I said I would. I explained how I took a small tree sapling with me and we planted it in the garden. "A reminder of Mr Whiskers," I'd called it.

Isaac was quiet and a little out of sorts. He walked over to me with his head down, fisted my shirt and put his forehead on my shoulder. "You're a good man," he murmured.

I ran my hands through his hair and pulled him against me, kissing the side of his head. Something was eating at him, something was on his mind.

And maybe it was the wrong time, and I shouldn't have said anything, but I took his face in my hands and whispered, "I love you."

And he froze.

I could see the rapid rise and fall of his chest, and then he took a small step back. His mouth opened and closed, and I thought for a brief, wonderful moment he was about to tell me he loved me too.

But he didn't.

"Oh."

That's what he said. Oh.

"Carter, I—"

"It's okay, Isaac," I said quietly. "It doesn't matter if you don't love me back. I just wanted you to know."

He swallowed hard and shook his head. "I um, I… can't…"

He *can't*. I suddenly felt very stupid. How could I not have seen that coming? He couldn't allow himself to love Brady, how was he ever going to love me?

"I should go," I said softly. I was embarrassed, and quite frankly, I felt like I'd been punched in the stomach. I felt nauseous. "I'll call you. I, um… Just give me some time," I told him, pulled my keys out of my pocket and walked around him toward the front door.

"Carter, please…"

"Don't," I told him. *Don't make it worse. Don't pity me. Don't tell me you never thought of me like that. Don't tell me you just want to be friends. Just don't.* "Please don't. Of course you can't do this. I should have known. Isaac, I... I'll call you," I told him again, and I left.

I wasn't sure when I'd call him or what I'd say. I needed a day or two to get my head around what had just happened, some time to lick my wounds, so to speak.

I got home in a daze, and with no appetite for dinner, I walked Missy, then fell into bed around midnight and stared at the wall 'til God-knows-when. I got to work early and it wasn't long after, my cell phone buzzed in my pocket.

His name flashed across the screen. Isaac.

But I couldn't answer it. I wasn't ready to hear goodbye. I needed more time. I knew I shouldn't blame him. It was hardly his fault. But I still did; a small part of me did blame him. It was easier than wearing the blame myself.

Because if I'd kept my mouth shut, everything would still be great.

Except it wouldn't.

Because now I knew.

And by the time our last patient walked out the door, it was near dark and I'd missed three calls from Isaac. He left three messages. The first was, "Carter, we need to talk. Please call me." The second was, "Carter, please." The third was just a quiet click in my ear.

So when I was sitting at my work desk and my phone rang the fourth time, I checked the screen, even though I had no intention to answer it. I was expecting to see Isaac's name, but it wasn't. It was Hannah.

I pressed the button to answer. "Hi, Hannah." My voice sounded distant, even to me.

"Carter," she said, relieved. "I was beginning to worry."

I smiled sadly. "Work's been busy, sorry." Then I wondered if something had happened with Brady. "Is Brady okay?"

"Brady's fine," she said. "Isaac's not though. What the hell happened between you?"

"What do you mean Isaac's not? Is he okay?"

"Physically, he's fine," she told me. "Well, he would be if he took his head out of his ass."

I huffed out a laugh, relieved. She sure had a way with words.

"But he's miserable," she added quietly. "He won't tell me what happened. Carter, he never doesn't tell me stuff, just that you won't take his calls. So please, what did he do?"

I sighed. "It's not his fault."

"What did he do?" she asked again. "He's miserable, you're miserable, and he's hiding in his room. In bed, under the covers, I think. He's got guilty written all over him."

I pressed my thumb and forefinger into my eyes, and sighed. "I told him I loved him."

Hannah was silent for a moment. "And?"

"And nothing, he doesn't love me back," I said flatly.

"Did he say that?"

"Well, no," I admitted. "He didn't have to. His face told me all I needed to know."

"But he does, Carter," she said seriously. "He does love you. I know he does."

"Apparently not, Hannah. He said he *can't*," I said quietly. "Look, thanks anyway, but I gotta go."

"Please don't give up on him," she said, almost desperately. "He's scared, and he's stubborn. If you want, I'll drag his sorry ass down to see you right now."

I smiled, despite my mood. "Thanks, Hannah, but that won't be necessary. I don't think I'm ready to hear what he wants to tell me, but tell him I'll call him in a day or two. I need some time, okay?" Then I added, "Thank you, Hannah, for everything."

*Blind Faith*

When I got home, I took Missy for our usual walk, picked at something to eat and, after not sleeping much the night before, I crashed.

I wasn't sure what to do with my weekend. It was supposed to be raining on Saturday, so I figured I'd head back to work, but the weather would be clear on Sunday, so I thought I'd find that hiking trail Isaac had talked about.

I got into work on Saturday early, caught up on paperwork, then did stock inventory and it wasn't until lunchtime that I checked my phone. No missed calls. No messages. The one thing worse than Isaac calling me three times, was Isaac not calling me at all.

I threw my phone onto my desk and picked at my sandwich until I pushed it away too. My door was open, but Rani knocked anyway. She smiled. "You okay?" she asked, concerned.

I gave her a smile. "Yeah, I'm okay."

She didn't look convinced. Instead, she took a step into my office. "You seem distracted and sad," she said cautiously. "I just thought it might have something to do with Isaac Brannigan?"

My eyes snapped to hers. "Why would you think that?"

She smiled knowingly. "Because he's in the waiting room."

My eyes widened. "He's here?"

Rani smiled and nodded. "He phoned the front desk earlier and asked if you were on call. I said no, but you were here anyway, and asked if another doctor could help him. He said no and hung up. Then he turns up, says it's not an emergency, Brady's fine, but he wants to speak to you anyway." Then she smiled sadly. "You should see him. He's um, well, he's... you know it's raining outside, right?"

"Sure," I told her, not really sure what she meant. I

couldn't get my head around him being here. Fuck. He was here. He just couldn't wait. No time like the present to have your heart handed to you. I sighed and stood up. "Thanks, Rani."

"I can bring him down here, to your office, if you'd prefer the privacy?" she asked, seemingly aware this was a personal visit and apparently okay with the fact it was between two men.

I thought about it, where I wanted to have this conversation, but figured it didn't really matter. "It's okay. I'll come out to see him."

I walked up the corridor, steeling my resolve to tell him he was off the hook and I'd stop bothering him, and then I saw him. He sat there, in the waiting room, with Brady at his feet, both of them completely and utterly soaked to the bone.

Oh, God. My heart squeezed in my chest. "Isaac?"

He turned to the sound of my voice and stood up.

"You're drenched!"

"It's raining outside," he said. "I took the bus, so I had to walk a block."

Rani sighed beside me, with a *that's so sweet* look on her face. I shook my head at this impossible man, walked over to him, and put his hand on my arm. "Come this way," I said, leading him to an examination room.

As soon as the door was shut behind us, I let him have it. "What the hell were you thinking?"

He flinched at my tone. "You wouldn't take my calls."

"It's raining and cold outside, Isaac," I stated the obvious. "Why didn't you get Hannah to drive you?"

He shrugged. "We had a fight."

I sighed and pulled at my hair. Shaking my head, I walked over to the supplies shelf and grabbed some towels. And he just stood there, wet, looking very out of place and vulnerable. I walked back to him, slowly took off his sunglasses and dried his face, then ran the towel over his hair. And he let me. Normally so adamant to prove his independence, yet he stood there while I dried him.

But then he shivered.

"I need to get you home. You're freezing," I told him. Then I looked at an equally soaked Brady. "Both of you." I dried Brady as much as I could and when I was done, I handed Isaac his sunglasses.

He put them back on the exam table and grabbed my arm, looking at me with his blue un-seeing eyes. "Carter, please stop."

"Isaac, it's okay," I said weakly. "About the other night, I shouldn't have said anything. I'm sorry I ruined everything."

"What?" he asked. "No, Carter, no, don't be sorry. I'm the one who's sorry. I reacted terribly, and I wish I could take it back. I wish I could make it better." He shook his head. "Hannah told me she spoke to you, and how it sounded like a goodbye. Then she proceeded to tear shreds off me for being so horrible to you."

Oh, this just went from bad to worse. "So you're here now because Hannah made you feel bad?"

"No!" he cried. "Well, she said a lot of things that hit home, but she was right, and I'm so sorry, Carter. I never meant to hurt you. It was the last thing I wanted to do. You have to believe me. It's hard for me, but I'm trying," He was rambling, almost panicking. "I wish we could go back and do it over." His crystal blue eyes filled with tears. "I had to come to your work. I know it's not professional, but I've never been to your house. I couldn't have found it on my own, and you wouldn't take my calls. I was afraid I'd lose you."

My heart sank. "Isaac, I told you I loved you," I whispered. "And you rejected me. What was I supposed to think?"

His tears fell down his cheeks. "That I'm scared. That I don't want to lose you. That you're the best thing to ever happen to me." His face fell and he shrugged. "That I love you too."

"What?"

"Can you say it again?" he asked.

I shook my head. "Say what again?"

"Tell me you love me," he said, wiping his cheeks with his hands and ignoring my question. "Say it again, like you did the other night."

I shook my head. "Isaac, I don't think that's a good idea." I didn't think my heart could take it.

He frowned. "Please?" He reached out for me, his hands found my chest, then slid down my arms to my hands and he lifted them to his face. His hands were freezing. "We were like this, and you kissed my forehead," he said, and when he closed his eyes, fresh tears beaded on his eyelashes. "Please."

I leaned in, closed my eyes, and pressed my lips to his forehead.

His voice was just a whisper. "Then you told me you loved me."

"Isaac…"

"Please…" It was barely audible, and his hands gripped onto me as though he was scared I'd run. "Say it again. I want to make this right."

Although my heart told me not to do it, I figured I had nothing else to lose. So I closed my eyes, took a deep breath and murmured those words again. "I love you."

And he finally breathed, almost gasping for air, and he clung on to me, burying his face in my neck. "And I love you."

"Isaac?" I said softly, and pulled back to look at his face.

His eyes were closed, his forehead rested on mine, and he

murmured, "I love you," once more. "And I'm sorry. I'm so, so sorry."

I blinked. My head was spinning.

"That's what I should have said the first time," he said, his eyes were red and teary, and sadness was etched on his face. "I should have told you then. I shouldn't have been so scared, but I was. I still am. I'm so sorry I hurt you."

I answered by lifting his face and pressing my lips to his, kissing him softly. He gasped, but kissed me back, only pulling away so he could wrap his arms around me and hug me.

As I slid my arms under his jacket and around him, I could feel how wet and cold he was, and he shivered against my warmth. "Isaac," I said, pulling out of his embrace. "We're going to talk about this, but right now, I'm taking you home."

He was still shivering, but he nodded. I gave him back his sunglasses, picked up Brady's harness, gave the gorgeous dog a good pat, threw the wet towels in the dirty linen hamper, and led him out. I told Rani, who grinned when she saw us walk out with Isaac's hand on my arm, that I was taking Isaac and Brady home.

I left Isaac under the awning so I could get Brady harnessed in to the backseat of my Jeep, and then, by the time I raced back in the pouring rain to lead Isaac over, I was almost as wet as they were. I cranked up the heat, and, instead of taking them back to Isaac's place, I took them to mine.

"Why are we going to your house?" Isaac asked. "We never go to your house."

So I told him. "Because I've got a wood fire, and Brady needs to get warm."

"Oh," Isaac said, trying to hide his chattering teeth. Then he asked quietly, "Will he be okay?"

"I'm sure he'll be fine," I told him.

"I didn't realize it was so cold."

"Isaac, it's almost winter!"

"I know," he said, shaking his head. "I just didn't think. I needed to speak to you, and I just didn't think."

I sighed, as I pulled up in front of my place. "Come on, we'll get you inside."

I held Isaac's arm, guiding him up my front steps. "There are six steps," I told him. "Then a little porch and another step inside. It's a little bungalow style house," I added, thinking he could use a visual image of where he was.

I opened the door, and Missy greeted us, apparently with even more enthusiasm to see Brady over me. I led Isaac down the hall, explaining as I went. "I'm putting you in the shower to warm you up, and while you're in there, I can start the fire for Brady."

My bathroom was small compared to Isaac's. I showed him where the vanity was, the toilet and then the shower. "Taps at twelve o'clock, soap at nine o'clock. When you get out, your towel will be on the rail here." I showed him with his hand. "I'll be just down the hall, holler if you need me."

He toed off his shoes, and I took them and his jacket to dry by the fire. His clothes were soaked, so I added, "I'll bring in a change of clothes. I'll leave them on the vanity."

"Okay," he said quietly. "Thank you, Carter."

I turned the taps on for him, letting the hot water run. I pecked his lips with mine. "You're welcome."

∽

I'd changed into dry clothes and had the fire started nicely when Isaac called out to me. I walked into the bathroom and smiled. I'd given him some sweatpants along with my old UConn sweatshirt, and I had to admit, I liked to see him in it.

I took his hand and led him to the living room. "The dogs have taken pole position in front of the fire," I told him. "So we get the sofa."

As we sat down, he turned his face toward the fireplace, obviously feeling the warmth on his skin, listening to the sounds of it, or rain in a strange house. Possibly both. "How's Brady?"

"He's fine. Almost asleep," I reassured him. "I think he was just waiting to see you before he closed his eyes."

Isaac nodded, but said nothing. He fidgeted and cleared his throat. "So you, um, wanted to talk?"

"Yes, I think we need to," I told him. I took a deep breath. "Isaac, I won't lie, I was very hurt. It wasn't easy for me to just come out and say those words to you."

"I know, and I'm sorry," he said, for the twentieth time.

"Stop apologizing," I told him. "I know you didn't mean it."

His voice was so quiet, I barely heard him. "Did you still mean them?"

I laughed and took his hand, lifting it to my lips. "You silly man, of course I still mean them. I'm not the kind of guy who falls in love every other day, so for as long as you want, you're stuck with me."

He smiled sadly. "I don't want you to leave me."

I swung one leg around him, maneuvering us so he was between my legs and pulled him against me." Then don't push me away."

He snuggled into me, holding me tight and was quiet for a long moment. I asked him if he was warm enough.

"Yeah, thank you." He nodded, then he pulled out of my arms and sat up straight. "Carter, can I ask something of you?"

"Of course."

"Please don't ignore my phone calls." He spoke with his head bowed, and he swallowed loudly. "If you're mad at me, then answer the phone and tell me you are, yell at me, tell me I'm being an ass, or whatever." Then he added softly, "It's bad enough I don't have sight, I can't deal with silence too."

Oh, Isaac. "I'm sorry," I told him sincerely. "I didn't think of it like that. I didn't answer your calls because I didn't want to hear you say goodbye." I pulled him against me and kissed him. "I still can't believe you walked in the rain to come find me."

"I'm trying, Carter," he said quietly. "I am. This is new for me, and it's not easy. You know why…" he sighed sadly. "But I want this. I want to love you, as much as it scares me."

"I want you to love me, too."

His hands held my face, and then slowly, gently, he started to kiss me. It was different somehow, more tender, more serious. And I knew this was it. I wanted him. I wanted to show him how much I loved him.

I pulled his face into my hands and whispered against his lips. "Isaac, I want to take you to bed."

Knowing exactly what I meant, he exhaled in a rush, and nodded. "Yes."

I led him to my room and gently helped him onto my bed. I crawled up his body, settling between his legs, and pressed my weight on his. Then I kissed him, for all I was worth. I wrapped my arms around him, rocked my hips into him, and entwined my tongue with his.

He was soon writhing and begging, and when I had him naked and ready for me, I asked him one final time if this was what he wanted. His hands touched the sides of my face, and he nodded.

"Please."

I leaned over him, pushing his legs up higher, open wider, held his face and kissed him. "Tell me if I hurt you."

And I pushed myself inside him, slowly, oh-so-slowly. So tender, so tight, and so, so good.

He gasped, his fingers digging into my skin, his eyes were closed tight and he groaned, "Oh, fuck."

I held his face, trying not to push inside him too hard, too much. "Are you okay?"

He gasped again and nodded. "Yes, Carter. Oh, my God," he breathed the words, and his fingers dug into me.

I started to move then, pushing all the way in, making him gasp and moan. I leaned up on one hand and took his cock in my other hand, stroking and squeezing him while I was buried inside him.

I wanted to make this good for him, his first time. I wanted him to feel how good it could be, how good I could make him feel. I wanted his body to know my body, how it felt against him, inside him. I wanted to give him pleasure like he'd never known.

Keeping my fingers wrapped around his length, I leaned down and kissed his mouth, his neck. I whispered sweet words of nothing, hot in his ear, making him shudder and moan. I wanted to encompass him, surround him. I wanted him to feel everything. I worshipped his body with my mouth, my hands, and my cock.

And then his body could take no more. He bucked his hips, his mouth fell open in a silent scream, his un-seeing so-blue eyes went wide, and he came.

His whole body shook and trembled under me, around me, where I was buried inside him. I slid my arms around him, holding onto him as wave after wave wracked through him, his orgasm spilling between us.

Pleasure so intense, so pure, ripped from my bones and

my skin, surging, filling the condom deep inside him. With no sense of being, there was only him, his body, his arms around me. And when I floated back into my body, his fingers were tracing circles on my back.

I pulled out of him, but his arms tightened around me, like he didn't want me to move. I held him for a long time, completely wrapped up in each other, neither of us speaking, just touching with fingers and soft lips.

Eventually, I asked him, "Are you okay?"

He nodded, and I could feel him smile into my neck. "Better than okay."

"How about we get cleaned up, order in some pizza and spend the night in front of the fire?"

"Sounds perfect."

## 11

This time I showered with him, cleaning him, soaping him, running my hands all over him, making him laugh. "We'll end up back in bed if you don't quit doing that," he said.

"I wouldn't mind," I told him, playfully biting the back of his neck.

When we were done and dinner was ordered, I showed him around my house. "It's small, but I needed a house with a decent yard for Missy," I explained. "As it turns out, I'm not here much."

I was standing behind him, with my hands over his, moving them, allowing him to feel all along the kitchen counter. I showed him where the coffee machine was, the sink, the microwave. I didn't need to stand behind him like that, but he didn't mind. He didn't mind at all.

Because when I stood behind him like that, I could kiss his neck and press myself against him. No, he didn't mind at all.

"Should we just go back to bed?" he asked with a laugh.

I kissed his neck again, then turned him so he faced me.

"Don't tempt me," I said with a kiss, gently pulling on his bottom lip with mine, and then the doorbell rang. I groaned. "That's dinner."

He smiled. "Don't sound so disappointed."

After we ate and were snuggled on the sofa, I picked up my cell phone. "We should call Hannah."

"Why?"

"Because she'll be worried about you."

He sighed. "She won't want to talk to me. I said some less-than-pleasant things to her."

I withheld a sigh. Of course he'd said some less-than-pleasant things to her. Instead, I kissed the side of his head. "Of course she'll want to talk to you. She might not be too happy with you, but she loves you." I pressed her number and handed the phone to him.

I could hear her voice. Obviously having seen my number come up on her screen, she answered with a cautious, "Carter?"

"No, it's me, Isaac."

I went into the kitchen and grabbed some bottled water, giving him privacy to speak to his sister, though I could still hear his side of the conversation. "No, we're at his place... He's here too..." I presumed he was talking about Brady. "... No, I went to his work... Yes, Hannah, in the rain... He said the same thing... I'm fine... Yes..." he smiled into the phone, "...Yes, I told him I loved him... It went very well... Yes, *that* well... No, I'm not telling you that!"

I chuckled at his side of the conversation, having a pretty good idea what Hannah just asked him. I sat beside him again, sliding a leg in behind him and he quickly nestled himself back into me.

"Um, hang on I'll ask," he said to his sister. Then he asked me, "What are we doing tomorrow?"

*Blind Faith*

"Hiking."

"Hiking," he repeated into the phone then he stopped. "Hiking?"

I chuckled. "Yep, I was going to check out that Wompatuck State Park trail you mentioned. If the weather's good, there's no reason why we still can't."

He chatted with Hannah for a little while, he apologized for the horrible things he said, she apologized for the same, and then he handed my phone back to me.

"Thank you."

He wasn't thanking me for the use of my phone. He was thanking me for making him call his sister. "You're more than welcome."

He leaned his head back on my chest and smiled.

~

I got up early, let the dogs out for a pee, put some more wood on the fire and climbed back into bed, sliding right up close to him. Isaac was warm and he grumbled when I put my cold feet on him, making me smile. But he wrapped his arms around me as he came to grips with the world.

"Good morning."

"Yes, it is." His arms tightened. "Did you start the coffee machine?"

"Oh, I forgot," I told him. "I put the dogs out and stoked the fire, but no coffee."

Then he tried to push me out of bed. "Out you go. Coffee for me, or no cuddles for you."

I laughed, but snuck back in and wrapped my arms around him tight. His arms wrapped warmly around me and he sighed. "Is it hiking weather?" he asked. "Or is it stay-in-bed-all-day weather?"

I chuckled. "Well, it's a clear sky if that's what you're asking."

"That's a shame."

I slid my hand down over his ass and gave it a good squeeze. "If we go hiking early enough, then we'll be back by lunch."

"And we can spend all afternoon in bed?"

"I've created a monster!" I said with a laugh. "Yes, all afternoon in bed, all night too, if you want."

He sat up. "Right, then let's go! The sooner we leave, the sooner we get back!" he ordered. I laughed and he picked up a pillow and hit me with it. He really did have good aim for a blind guy.

"Come on, Mr Insatiable, you have the first shower, I'll start the coffee."

~

Wompatuck State Park wasn't actually too far a drive. Another ten or so miles past the animal hospital, and considering I'd never been there and had a blind man as my navigator, I think we did quite well. But as I pulled up at the reserve, it occurred to me we should have taken the bus. Next time, I thought. Next time we come up here, we'd catch the bus so if Isaac ever decided he wanted to come up here without me, Brady would be familiar.

Then there wouldn't be a repeat of yesterday, and Isaac walking one block too many in the rain. And he'd be doing something with Brady. I smiled at the thought.

"Wow," I muttered, getting out of my Jeep. "It really is pretty."

Isaac harnessed Brady and said, "There are two trails off

*Blind Faith*

to the far end." He gave a pointed nod to the right. "They lead down through the woods to the lake. The sounds down there are amazing. Birds, water, cicadas, more birds, it's incredible."

I clicked the leash on Missy and smiled. "Then we'll go there first."

"You'll have to help guide me," he told me. "When I came here before, with Rosie, I'd also have my cane. Plus Brady's never been here before."

So that's exactly what we did. We took our time, walking the trail down to the small lake. I guided as well as I could, and Brady was outstanding. It was one thing to see Brady on flat surfaces, on the street and navigating traffic, but to see him on nature trails with uneven footing, tree roots as steps and slippery ground was something else. How he'd stop, start, turn, nudge.

He was a remarkable animal.

For a remarkable human being.

And when we walked back, we sat on a park bench. I handed Isaac a bottle of water, got out my transportable doggie water dish and gave the two dogs a drink too. After watching Isaac and Brady work so well together, so seamlessly, I expected Isaac to give Brady a pat, or some recognition, or something.

Anything.

But he didn't. Nothing.

Instead, he talked of other times he'd been here, with Rosie. He smiled when he talked, and as much as I wanted to say something, I didn't. After the last few days, with our declarations of love, miscommunications, fighting, and making up, I just didn't want to ruin it. I didn't want to spoil it.

I wanted to tell him that Brady was just as fantastic as

Rosie. I wanted to tell him if he didn't stop and notice, he'd miss out on knowing this wonderful, wonderful dog.

But I didn't.

And I knew damn well you weren't supposed to touch a guide dog when it was working, if it was harnessed, but I had to acknowledge him. I had to let him know he'd done well, that he was appreciated, loved. The vet in me, the animal lover in me, couldn't just sit there and watch this beautiful dog, with his big brown eyes, just sit there, waiting for some kind of recognition. So with the pretense of collecting the water dish, I ruffled the fur on his forehead.

If Isaac somehow knew, with his uncanny ability to know without seeing, he didn't let on. He never said a word.

But Brady looked up at me, with his tongue lolling out the side of his mouth and his happy brown eyes smiling, and I grinned right back at him.

We stayed in the warmth of the winter sun, sitting on the park bench, and I described what I saw. There was an amenities block that looked kind of new, new signs to say which trails suited which types of hikers and new picnic tables. I imagined in summer it would be very busy, but as the seasons got colder, not so many people went hiking.

"I'd really like to come back," I said. "I'd like to take some other trails, so next weekend, if the weather's clear, we could come back, yeah?"

"Sure," Isaac said. "We could do one more trail today if you really wanted."

"No," I said, standing up. "I promised you an afternoon of indoor activities, and I intend to keep that promise."

Isaac smiled. "Indoor activities?"

"Yep," I said with a smile. "In bed, on the sofa, against the kitchen counter, in the shower..." I trailed off suggestively.

"In that order?"

*Blind Faith*

I laughed and pulled him to his feet. "Anything you want."

"Well, I want," he said, standing up close to me, he inhaled deeply, running his nose up my neck, breathing in my scent. "In that order. Twice."

I groaned out a laugh and palmed the sudden ache in my groin. "Then we'd better leave."

I picked up my backpack and handed Brady's harness handle to Isaac. I looked at the two dogs. "Come on, kids, we ready to leave?"

"Um," Isaac asked. "You just called the dogs 'kids', didn't you?"

I grinned. "Yep."

He shook his head at me and as he was getting into the Jeep, he said, "Oh, shoot!"

"What's up?"

"Next weekend," he started. "I can't go hiking with you. We're having a working bee at the school next weekend."

"A working bee?"

"Yeah, you know, yard cleaning, gardening, tidying up, maintenance, pruning trees, that kind of thing?"

"Pruning trees?" I asked. "I don't mean to be rude, but how does a blind person prune a tree?"

Isaac clicked in his seatbelt. "I have no clue. To be honest, I don't even know if we have trees, but I sure as hell hope we do."

I smiled, almost afraid to ask. "Why?"

"Because last year, Mr Grainger, the art teacher, took pruning shears to something."

I laughed. Every now and again, I would see his sense of humor, just like Hannah's, and I hoped it was something he'd show me more often. "Isaac, did you just make a blind joke?"

He grinned. "No, Mr Grainger really did take the secateurs to something. Or so I was told. But they hid the gardening equipment after that, now no one can find it."

I cracked up laughing, and Isaac chuckled. I lifted his hand to my lips and kissed his knuckles. "Can I come along?" I asked. "To the working bee?"

"Sure," he said, still smiling. "You can look for the pruning shears."

∼

I was really looking forward to seeing where Isaac worked. I wanted to know where he spent his days, what he did, why he loved it. I'd heard so much about it, and he'd shown me the work he brought home, but it was in Braille, so I really had no idea what it was. I mean, I was learning, but it was like another language, and quite frankly, it was confusing. I couldn't imagine him learning this as a small boy. And every time I watched him read, he just amazed me even more.

We had Brady with us, of course, but Missy had to stay at home. And, as Isaac harnessed his dog in the parking lot, he asked me, "Can I introduce you as my boyfriend?"

I smiled. "Of course you can."

He grinned. "A lot of them don't know I'm gay," he went on to say. "So I want graphic details of facial expressions, please."

I laughed at him. "Oh, my God."

He smiled and started walking toward the building. "Are you coming?"

He was still smiling as he walked in. The building itself, the classrooms, the setup, was amazing. I could see why Isaac loved it here—he'd spent years here, first being taught, then teaching—and I felt a pang of sadness that he had never seen it.

*Blind Faith*

It was just like a school, which kind of surprised me. There were posters on walls, student projects on display, notices on boards—some in writing, some in Braille—there were classes off corridors and, upon first impression, I wouldn't have guessed it was a school for the blind.

It wasn't until I looked a little closer, saw the equipment, saw the Braille templates on desks and saw the Braille written under all door signs and information plaques that I could see it was a school with a purpose. And I realized just what it was Isaac did every day.

He gave kids purpose.

"Wow," I said softly. "It looks like a normal school, with all the posters and boards."

Isaac grinned. "Not all students and teachers are completely blind. The posters are for them, as well as visitors like you."

"Not at all," I answered quickly. "It's just... Isaac, this place is amazing."

He was still smiling. "Is it?"

"Hi, Isaac," an older woman called out as she walked down the corridor. "So glad you could come today." She turned and looked at me from the corner of her eye. It was obvious she could see, just somewhat limited. "So, who have you brought with you today?"

"Marianna Turis," Isaac called her by her full name. "I'd like you to meet Carter Reece."

"Ah," she said knowingly. "You're the Carter I've been hearing about."

It surprised me that she'd heard of me. "All good stories, I hope."

She smiled. "Oh, yes. Isaac talks very highly of you."

Not allowing me to enjoy that compliment for long, Isaac

said, "Carter, Marianna is the Dean of our wonderful school. She's the boss, the one who keeps us busy."

"Well, I try," she said with a smile. "Where's Hannah?"

"She's spending the weekend away with her husband," Isaac told her. "She thought, because I was bringing Carter here today, she wouldn't be needed, so they left this morning for a small getaway."

"Oh, good for her," she said warmly. It was obvious they liked each other. "Now, I must keep going. Carter, it was nice to finally meet you."

"Yes, nice to meet you too," I said, a little baffled.

When she'd gone, and we were alone in the hall, I whispered, "I thought no one knew."

"No one but her," Isaac said with a smile. "I've known her since I was about eight. We talk about most things. She's known I was gay for as long as I have."

And he wasn't kidding when he said he'd introduce me as his boyfriend. That's exactly what he did. There were a few surprised reactions, mostly of the "shocked silence" kind, but I got the feeling Isaac couldn't have cared less.

It was as though he was proud to call me his boyfriend, like he cared about my feelings more than their opinions. His boss knew, had always known apparently, and that was all that mattered.

I spent most of the day with Isaac, some of it outside helping others, and I realized it really wasn't about maintenance at all. It was about community. It was about these people, their friends and families, getting together to do something constructive. It was great.

Once most people had established the three basic points of conversation with me—that my name was Carter Reece, yes, I'm a vet, and yes, I'm here with Isaac—they really only mostly cared that I was handy with a shovel and a paintbrush.

## Blind Faith

When we stopped for lunch, Isaac said he wanted to show me something. I followed him into one of the classrooms. "You wanted to see what I do?" he asked rhetorically. "Well, this is my main room."

It was a large room, and besides the tech stuff like screens with audio equipment, there were posters on the wall with big writing and Braille placards, and pictures and colorful handprints. But the tiny desks were the giveaway.

"Is this the elementary room?"

Isaac smiled. "It's where I teach the youngest kids, yes," he explained. "Ages range from six to ten." He stood at the front of the room, like he would if his students were there.

I looked around, taking in the room he was obviously proud of. "What are these?" I asked, walking to the side wall. "These display cards with stuff all over them. Is that sand?"

Isaac smiled. "Yes. Not all kids are completely blind, some are, but they're all tactile. Each of them learn by touch. So when we're reading new books, we'll set up display cards with the description word in Braille, but then we'll have the items in a box in front of it, or stuck to the poster, so the kids can learn the word, but also learn what it feels like."

There were seashells, sand, straw, leaves, grass, and dirt. I could just imagine the kids feeling the different textures of things from the books they're reading. "This is fantastic, Isaac." Then I saw the new, only half done display. "Cotton wool and fake fur," I said with a smile. "Is that for the book Peter Rabbit?"

Isaac grinned. "Yes, see the pot of dirt?"

There was a small tub of dirt on the shelf. "Yeah."

"We're growing carrots," he said, smiling and shaking his head. "They wanted to plant an entire vegetable patch."

I smiled. "Isaac, it's just amazing. You're amazing."

"Hardly."

"It's true!" I told him. "You don't just teach these kids to read. You make the book real, you bring it to life for them."

He smiled. "I just want them to enjoy it."

And then I had an idea. "Isaac, if it's all right with you, I could bring in some real rabbits. The kids could pet them, hold them."

Isaac's expression was one of almost disbelief. "You'd do that?"

"Of course I would," I told him. "If it's okay with your boss, or whoever you need to ask. We have a lady at work who breeds dwarf lop-eared rabbits. She brought them in just last week. I'm sure if I asked her, told her what it was for, she wouldn't mind."

"Oh, Carter," he said quietly. "The kids would love that."

I grinned. "I would too."

## 12

Seeing Isaac at his job that weekend for the working bee really put him in another light for me. But seeing him at work with the kids he taught was something very special.

We got permission for me to bring in some rabbits, so I cleared my appointments at the animal hospital one afternoon and took in two of the cutest little bunnies for his class.

"We have a very special guest today, with a very special surprise," Isaac told the kids. There were eight children, like he'd said, varying in ages of six to about ten. Some of them were like Isaac, their eyes looked completely normal and some looked obviously blind, but they all had smiles the size of Texas. Brady was lying down at Isaac's desk. He looked up and thumped his tail when he saw me.

"This is Dr Reece, and he's a veterinarian," Isaac explained to the class. "He looks after animals."

"Good afternoon, boys and girls," I said.

"Now class, what book have we been reading?"

"*The Tales of Peter Rabbit*," one of the older girls answered.

"Very good, Georgia," Isaac said, recognizing her from her voice alone.

"So," Isaac said with a smile, "what kind of animal do you think Dr Reece might have brought in for us today?"

"A rabbit!" a few of them answered together.

Their excitement was palpable. They squealed, chatted, and somehow, their grins grew even wider. We had them sit on the floor in a sort-of circle, and I took one little dwarf lop-eared Peter Rabbit out of the carry-crate. I walked up to Isaac and said softly, "Here, hold this one. Keep him against your body."

Isaac put his hands up to his chest, and I handed over the little rabbit. It wasn't much bigger than his hand. "Keep a hold of his back feet like this," I said, taking his hand in mine and moving it so he held the rabbit properly. "He's only little, but he's got strong hind legs."

Isaac smiled. "He's so soft."

I grinned back at him. "He sure is."

Isaac sat with the kids, letting them each feel the soft fur, the soft ears, the twitching nose and the little cotton tail. I knelt down with the other, more docile rabbit, letting the kids each have a turn holding it.

The looks on their faces, their smiles, were beautiful.

When they'd each had a hold, I put the rabbits back in the carry-crate, and that's when the questions started. What kind of animals did I look after? What's the biggest animal I'd ever treated? What was the smallest? Did I have a pet monkey?

I laughed. "No, I don't have a pet monkey." Then I told them, "I have a dog. Her name is Missy, and she's black and white with long fur that I have to brush nearly every day."

"Like hair?"

I chuckled. "Yes, just like your hair."

"Is she pretty?" One little girl asked. "Do you put bows in her hair?"

I smiled. "She's pretty without bows," I answered.

"Can she do tricks?"

"Some," I said. "She can sit, stay, roll over, fetch."

A little boy with really thick glasses asked, "Do you look after other dogs like Mr Brannigan's Brady?"

"Actually, Brady is the first guide dog I've ever treated," I told them. "And he's the cleverest dog I've ever met."

"Is he cleverer than Missy?" the younger girl asked.

"Yes, much cleverer. Brady is a very special dog, who has a very special job," I said. "I think Brady is by far the most special dog I've ever met."

And then I looked at Isaac.

He looked... shocked, I think. But mostly he looked peeved. His face was turned, as though he was rejecting the sound of my voice, and I could see his jaw was clenched. Fuck.

"Okay," I said to the class. "I've had the best time visiting, but I better get the rabbits home."

Isaac stood across from me, putting a very discernible distance between us. Not that I expected him to stand right up close to me, but he stood just about as far from me as he could, and his arms were crossed. And without a word, his body language told me I'd crossed some invisible line. He instructed the class to thank me, which they did, and then he basically dismissed me.

I took the rabbits back to their owner, told her she'd just made eight kids very happy, and then I went back to work. I stayed later than I needed to, but got caught up on some paperwork I'd missed by visiting Isaac at school.

So his mood swung on a dime at the mere mention of what a good dog Brady was. I thought of all the times I'd almost asked him why he didn't show the dog any affection, any recognition, and was sadly relieved I'd never mentioned it.

My first reaction was to back off and give him space. It had always been my initial, knee-jerk reaction to retreat and regroup. It always had been. I hated confrontation and avoided it at all costs. So if it were up to me, I'd give him space until he wanted to talk.

But he can't deal with silence. That's what he'd told me. *It was bad enough he didn't have sight, he couldn't deal with silence too.* That's what he'd said.

So I picked up my phone and called him. I knew he'd be home by then, I knew he'd hear his phone and I knew the synthetic voice on his phone would tell him it was me calling. But still he didn't answer.

So much for not dealing well with silence.

I tried his number again before I took Missy for a walk and again when our walk was done. But when I called again before I went to bed and he still didn't answer, I left a less than impressed message.

"You tell me you can't deal with silence, but what you should have said was, you just can't deal with it when it's directed *at* you. You seem to be able to *give* it just fine. So, you wanted to know when I'm mad at you, or when you're being an ass, well guess what? I'm mad and you're an ass."

The voicemail cut me off, which just pissed me off even more. So I called back, and of course, it went to voicemail. "You know, I wasn't mad at you earlier, but I am now. You're giving me the silent treatment after you specifically asked me not to do the same. Why what I said pissed you off, I'll never know, but how you're reacting is fucking childish."

After I'd paced the floor and pulled at my hair, grumbling the entire time to Missy that Isaac would be the death of me, then because I felt like a bastard, I called a third and final time and left a very quiet and equally simple, "I love you."

∼

Isaac called me before breakfast. "Can we talk?" he asked. "Can you come around after work?"

I sighed. "That depends. Is it a good 'we need to talk this through' talk, or is it a bad 'It's not you, it's me' kind of talk?"

He huffed out a laugh. "Are you still mad at me?"

"Yes," I answered quickly. Then I thought about it. Was I still mad at him? I sighed again. "No."

"Oh, Carter," he said softly. "You know what I love about you?"

I shook my head. God, this man was tiring. "To be honest, Isaac, I don't have a clue."

He chuckled. "I'll tell you if you come around after work."

I exhaled loudly and shook my head. "Are you trying to blackmail me?"

"Is it working?"

"Maybe." I smiled at this familiar conversation. "You're impossible."

"It's part of my charm."

I was smiling despite still being mad at him. "Okay, I'll come around after work."

He sighed in relief. "Thank you."

"And Isaac?"

"Yeah?"

"You need to work on your charm."

∼

I arrived at Isaac's just as Hannah was leaving, which I think was a deliberate ploy to speak to me alone.

As I got out of my Jeep, she smiled like always, but it was tinged with sadness. I gave her a nod, asked how she'd been, how Carlos was, what their plans were for this glorious, cold Friday night. We made general small talk, trying to ignore the inevitable.

Then she tilted her head and smiled at me. "I'm glad you came."

I leaned against my Jeep and nodded. "Hannah, I love your brother, but he's a moody bastard."

She laughed, like I'd just told her the sky was blue. Then she said, "He told me he made you mad." Her eyes softened. "He let me listen to your voice messages. They were sweet."

I was used to them having no secrets. I smiled. "He's infuriating."

She laughed and looked at me with warm eyes. "Don't let him get away with it."

I smiled at her. "I have no intention of letting him get away with anything."

Hannah grinned at me and fixed her scarf. "Go on inside, get out of this cold."

I walked inside and closed the door behind me. "Isaac?"

"In the kitchen."

I walked through, and there he was, sans sunglasses, standing at the stove, making what looked like dinner. "Hey," I said softly.

"Hey."

It was silent between us for a moment, neither of us sure what to say. He turned to stir the big pot on the stove, so I asked, "What are you cooking?"

He shrugged. "It's just a vegetable soup. I cut up some

*Blind Faith*

veggies, throw them in some stock, and boil. Even I can do it." Then he added, "Hannah tells me being blind or sighted wouldn't make any difference to my cooking. It's pretty bad apparently." He smiled sadly. "But veggie soup I can do."

I smiled. "Smells good."

"You're more than welcome to have some."

I didn't answer his offer of staying. Instead I took a deep breath and asked, "What did you want to talk about?"

He turned to face me and took a little while to speak. "I'm sorry about yesterday," he said quietly. "You went out of your way to come to the school, to bring rabbits for the kids, and I treated you terribly. I'm very sorry."

I sighed. "You really have apologizing down to an art, don't you?"

His face pinched. "I do it a lot," he confessed. "I'm quite obnoxious apparently, and have a tendency to be rude."

It sounded as though he was quoting Hannah. So I added, "You forgot moody."

"Oh, and moody."

I shook my head and smiled at him. "And handsome."

His smile died. "Do you forgive me?"

I took his hand. "You asked me to not give you the silent treatment, to answer your calls when you phone me, then you turn around and do the exact same thing. Isaac, that wasn't fair."

"I know, and I'm sorry."

"How about we aim for fewer arguments, fewer apologies, and aim at more telling me what's bothering you, or what I said that was so wrong?"

He nodded. "That sounds good."

"Will you tell me what I said yesterday in the classroom that upset you?"

Isaac hesitated. "Um, some days are easier than others.

Some things are unexpected and unnerving for me, and my temper gets the better of me." Then he added quietly, "You mentioned Brady…"

"And?"

He shrugged, not sure how to say whatever it was he was trying to say. "And I feel guilty…"

"Guilty?" I put my hands on his shoulders. "Isaac, you have no reason to feel any guilt for having another dog."

"I know, but some days I feel like I'm betraying what I had with Rosie." He shrugged again. "I can't help what I feel."

"I know, baby. And you're entitled to feel whatever you want, but I'm sure Rosie would understand," I said, pulling him against me. I wrapped my arms around him. He shrugged and said nothing, and I knew our conversation about Rosie or Brady was over, so I left well enough alone for the time being. It was a subject I knew we'd have to discuss at some point. When he was ready, we'd talk about it. But there was a small part of me that didn't want to push the issue before he was ready, because I didn't want to risk how far we'd come. He was opening up to me, slowly, but surely. Every day was a small accomplishment in unraveling the mystery that was Isaac Brannigan. So once again, I changed the subject.

"Of course I forgive you," I told him, then pulled his chin up so I could kiss him. "So now are you going to tell me what it is you love about me?"

He finally smiled. "That you don't treat me any different. That you treat me like you treat everyone else. You don't wrap me up in cotton wool, you don't make concessions for me, you don't try and do everything for me. You certainly don't take any of my crap," he said. Then he added quietly, "You don't treat me like I'm blind."

"It's never been an issue for me," I told him honestly. "I don't treat you any different because you're not any different."

Isaac smiled. "And that's why I love you."

I pulled him against me again, and for a long moment, we just stood in the kitchen and held each other. There was a push and pull with this man; he'd pull me in as though he couldn't live without me, and then push me away as though he didn't need me at all. I knew it was how he was learning to let me love him, and then a spike of fear would have him pushing me away again. He'd had so much loss in his life. I couldn't blame him for his reservations.

But his walls were slowly coming down. He'd just admitted to me he felt guilty for having Brady, like he was betraying the memory of his beloved Rosie. He'd basically admitted he loved Brady, and he was struggling to deal with how that made him feel about Rosie, the dog that saw him through some of the hardest times of his life.

Isaac's arms tightened around me. "Will you stay tonight?"

I pulled back and cupped his face in my hands. "I should go home. Missy's there, the house will be freezing without the fire going."

Keeping his hands on my sides, he rested his forehead against my cheek, and spoke to the floor. "You could go get her and come back." Then he said, "You wanted to go back to the Wompatuck trails. We could go tomorrow, spend the day like you wanted to."

I smiled and kissed the side of his head. I had no intention of staying, but to feel him in my arms, to feel him against me, melted my resolve. "Okay."

With his eyes closed and his hands fisting my shirt at my sides, he ran his nose along my jaw. "Don't take too long."

I lifted his face and kissed him deeply, sweeping my

tongue into his mouth, then slowly pulling his bottom lip in between mine. He moaned, and I smiled. "Hold that thought," I teased. "I'll be back soon."

He groaned this time, and as I pulled out my keys and walked to the door, he called out, "That's not fair!"

I laughed, and then smiled the whole way home. But I was back at his place in record time.

∼

He said he wanted to try something, and the shy, nervous way he asked me had my interest piqued.

We'd had dinner, and he had me pinned to the sofa, straddling my hips and kissing me.

"What is it?" I asked, too curious to hide my excitement.

He smirked shyly. "I'll show you." He swung his leg off me and stood up, taking my hand, and led me down the hall to his bedroom. He stopped at the foot of the bed and dropped my hand, but then he went to his dresser. "I have these," he said softly.

About a dozen different things flashed through my mind for what he could be talking about, but then he turned around and I saw what he had in his hands.

It was one of those black eye covers you see people wear when they sleep.

It was a blindfold.

"My shrink gave me a lot of these, for my family to wear," he said softly. "So they might be able to see what it was like for me."

"Isaac..."

"You don't have to wear it," he cut me off. "I just thought you might want to, you know, so you can see what it's like to explore, to have sex, by touch alone."

*Blind Faith*

Well, when he put it like that...

I took the blindfold and slipped the elastic over my head, fixing the soft padded eye covers in place. And my world was dark.

Isaac's hands went to my face, and his fingers deftly traced the blindfold ensuring it was on. And then he kissed me. Soft and slow, his mouth, his lips caressed me. He unbuttoned my shirt, kissing my neck as he went, pulled off my undershirt and ran kisses all over my chest.

He palmed my cock through my jeans, rubbing and squeezing, before pulling the button fly open. Tugging my jeans down, he took my length in his hand and wrapped his fingers around me.

All I could feel was his warm breath on my skin, his lips and his tongue when he licked my skin, the warmth of his fingers, his hand, as he pulled and squeezed. I could smell him, his scent, his deodorant. And when I touched him, ran my hands up his arms, down his sides, around his waist, over his ass, I could feel everything.

"Lie down," he instructed, his voice gruff. "Face down."

Fuck.

I knelt on the bed first, then lay down as he asked me to. I could hear him getting undressed. My skin felt alive, the anticipation sparked in every cell. I felt his hand on my foot, then the bed dipped and his hands ran slowly up my leg, then his mouth.

He licked, kissed, touched, traced, and pressed, and all I could do was feel. And listen. It's true that other senses are heightened when one is subdued, the sensations I felt were enhanced. Every touch, every movement, every sound.

His hands ran up the back of my thighs, and I could feel his breath there too, so his face was close to my skin. Then his hands ran over the flesh of my ass, kneading, gripping, and his lips, his mouth, kissed and he scraped his teeth against my skin. He spread my ass and then his tongue was there, warm and wet, as he licked me.

I'd rimmed him before, and he'd loved it, but he'd never done this to me before. I'd always been the one to take charge, to top him, to read his cues, to care for him. But he was in charge now, taking the lead.

I gripped the pillow, flooded with sensations, lifted my hips for him and spread my thighs. I wanted him. I wanted him inside me. And when he kissed up my spine and whispered behind my ear, "Carter, please?" I knew what he wanted.

"Yes," I whispered. "God, yes."

He leaned right over me, and I heard the bedside table drawer open. He never fumbled; he never hesitated. I heard the quiet rustle of foil, then he whispered, "Roll over, baby." And when I was on my back, he took my hand and gave me the condom and bottle of lube. "Hold these for me."

He maneuvered my legs so he was between my thighs, and he started by kissing my mouth, my neck, my chest, tracing his tongue over my nipples. His hands, his long fingers, felt every inch of skin, every muscle, every part of me. He worked a path down over my abs, my navel, lower, until his mouth found my aching cock.

Then his fingers were inside me, stretching me, the way I did him. Slow and sensual. I could feel everything. The way his fingers worked me, his mouth, and when I arched off the bed, shooting down his throat, he drank everything I gave him. Boneless, writhing, moaning, and somehow, I still needed more.

I lifted my heavy hand, still clutching the condom. "Please, Isaac."

*Blind Faith*

It had been a long time since I'd bottomed, and never with Isaac, but it was so right. I needed this. *We* needed this.

With the cover still over my eyes, he finally pushed inside me, and we moved as one, touching, holding. Both of us sightless, feeling, hearing everything. Everything. His pulse, his heartbeat, inside me, a part of me.

Then I felt the swell and surge of his cock inside me, I felt his body tremble and flex, and he whimpered the sweetest sound as he came.

He collapsed on top of me, murmuring words of love and heaven as his orgasm subsided. Without taking the blindfold off, I wrapped my arms around him, rolled us onto our sides, pulled the covers over us, and we slept.

∽

"I can't believe you're making us take the bus."

I smiled. "I can't believe you're still whining about it." Then I added, "At least you've stopped whining about the woolen beanie."

He turned his face toward me. "I must look like a douche."

"It's winter!" I said with a laugh. "Anyway, you look hot with your designer jacket, tight Armani shades and dark beanie."

"Hot?" he scoffed. Then he mumbled, "Oh, please."

I shook my head at him. "You have no idea how good looking you are. How hot you are. Girls, *and guys*, check you out all the time." Then I told him, "They look at me and must wonder what the hell someone like you is doing with someone like me."

"Then they see the guide dog," he mumbled quietly and frowned.

"Yes, then they see the guide dog, and *then* they understand what you're doing with me," I joked. But he didn't laugh. "Oh, come on, that was funny," I said with a nudge of my elbow. "Didn't you get it? They wonder what a cute guy like you is doing with me, then they see Brady and realize you're with me because you can't see what I look like?"

Isaac sighed. "I got the joke, Carter. It just wasn't funny."

"Then why are you trying not to smile?"

He shook his head, but his lips curled upward. "Your joke telling skills suck."

"You've never complained about my ability to suck before."

This time he laughed. "Promise me no more jokes."

Just then, a bus came into view. "This is our ride," I told him. As we climbed on and paid our fare, I realized just how daunting it must be for Isaac to simply get on a bus. A bus that could potentially take him anywhere, or drop him off God-only-knows where. I shuddered to think what would happen if he got on the wrong bus, got off at the wrong stop, or if some asshole followed him off the bus, thinking he was an easy target.

And all this time I'd thought Isaac had issues trusting people, when the truth was, he had more trust in people than I could fathom. He relied on the goodness of strangers, like a bus driver or a stranger on the bus, to tell him what route he was on, which stop to get off at. I imagined sitting on the bus with my eyes closed, having no idea of where I was, where I was going or even who was around me, and scared didn't begin to cover it.

He amazed me, this man beside me. His courage, his trust, his belief in himself, his bravery. I gave his hand a squeeze.

"You okay?" he asked me quietly, bringing my attention back.

"Of course," I told him.

"Do you think Missy will be okay?" he asked.

"Oh, sure," I told him. "She's probably already asleep on Brady's bed." Then I added, "Or yours."

The look on his face was priceless. I laughed, and he grumbled at me. "I thought I said no more jokes."

I grinned. "I wasn't joking."

◈

The park was perfect. The cooler weather meant there was less traffic, fewer people. We took the trail that led to the small lake, enjoying the seclusion, the silence. When we stopped for lunch, we sat at a picnic table with our backs resting against it, facing the water, and I described the scenery.

"There is a carpet of oranges, yellows and browns. The ground is covered with leaves. There are some trees with a little green, but not many. The water looks like dark glass." I sighed. "It's really pretty."

Isaac smiled. "Close your eyes." He waited a few seconds. "Are they closed?"

I chuckled. "Yes."

"Listen."

I took a deep breath and took in the world around me. At first all I could hear was the silence, but then other sounds trickled in. Birds, the far off sounds of some other hikers laughing, more birds, the leaves rustling, the gentle sounds of water.

Isaac asked quietly, "Can you hear it?"

"Sshhh."

He chuckled. "I told you."

I smiled. "It's magic, thank you," I said, not wanting to open my eyes. "Thank you for today, for showing me this place."

"The wind is getting cold," he said as though he'd spoken a thought out loud.

"Yeah," I agreed. "We'd better make a start on that other trail. What time did the bus driver say the last bus came back?"

"Four."

"We don't want to be here that long, do we?" I asked. "It'll be getting dark and cold by then."

Isaac nodded. "Yeah, God forbid it gets dark and I can't see where I'm going."

I laughed. "Okay, smartass. You know what I mean." I started to pack up our little picnic, giving Brady some more liver treats I'd brought for him, and while I was pretending to empty out his water dish, I gave him a quick pat.

Isaac stilled, as though he somehow knew I'd touched his dog. Maybe it jostled the harness or he heard it somehow or something. But he said nothing. He just turned, as though he couldn't believe I'd done it.

"We ready?" I asked, pretending to be oblivious.

He nodded and was quiet as we walked back along the trail to the main path, so I filled the void of silence, talking about everything Mark was up to until we reached the two far trails.

"Hey, babe," I said, looking up at the sky. "We might want to take the shorter trail so we make the earlier bus. There are some clouds coming in."

So we chose the shorter, easier trail, though it was still rugged enough. Nothing like what I was used to hiking back in Hartford, but still great nonetheless. The trail was really only wide enough for one person at a time, so Isaac and Brady went first and I followed closely.

We couldn't really talk as we hiked along the trail, as Isaac concentrated on his commands to his four-legged partner. I still marveled at the smarts of Brady. How he moved and how Isaac read his cues was just truly spectacular. As Isaac's boyfriend, someone who loved him, I knew Brady was special for the independence and security he gave Isaac, but add in the perspective of a vet, and I really found the dog extraordinary. I knew Brady had a purpose, a role to play. The logical part of my brain knew the dog had a job to do. Ultimately, it's the very reason why he was with Isaac.

But he was more than that.

He was a pet. He was a part of Isaac's family. And I just loved seeing them work together, as a team. As buddies.

And as we made it back to the main entrance and eventually fell on the seats to wait for the bus, I was still smiling. The cloud cover was coming in, it was expected to rain for most of the week, and there were even fewer people there now than there were earlier.

I handed Isaac his bottle of water, gave Brady a quick drink, and then, because I couldn't help myself, I gave him a good pat. I ruffled his ears, patted his neck. "You're such a good dog," I said, and got two smiling eyes and a side-lolling tongue as my thanks.

Isaac on the other hand, wasn't so grateful.

But I had to do something. I couldn't just sit there and watch this wonderful dog go unnoticed, unappreciated any longer. "Sorry, babe," I said to Isaac. "I know I'm not supposed to pat him when he's working, but he's not working right now, and he did *so* well today. He just amazes me, and you two are an awesome team."

Before he could say anything, the bus pulled in. I'd never

been a fan of public transport, but I'd never been so happy to see a bus. It saved me from the short-fused rant Isaac would no doubt serve me.

But he didn't. He sat on the bus with his head resting against the window, with his eyes closed.

"You okay?"

"Mm," he hummed. "Tired."

I nodded my understanding. No, there'd be no ranting, no spitfire temper. I was getting the silent treatment.

Fucking hell.

By the time we got back to his house, he still hadn't spoken. Maybe he was tired, though I doubted it. He unharnessed Brady and gave him fresh food and water, while I was met by a rather enthusiastic Missy. By the time we were both done, we met in the kitchen.

"Isaac, I'm sorry if what I said earlier about Brady upset you," I started. "But we promised to talk about this, remember?"

He shrugged. "I'm just tired all of a sudden, that's all."

I wasn't buying it. "Isaac—"

He cut me off. "I had a really good time today," he said flatly. "But I'm tired."

"Did you want me to run you a bath?"

"No, thanks," he said, shaking his head. "But could you set the alarm when you go, please?"

He was dismissing me. Without so much as a fucking explanation. "You know what?" I said curtly. "I had a really good time today too. Until now. Until you started giving me the silent treatment."

He turned his head, his jaw was clenched. But he said nothing.

I was so fucking mad at him. "Sure, I'll go. But Isaac, understand this," I said, grabbing my things. "Yes, I love you.

And I'm really fucking sorry to disappoint you, but I also love Brady. I love him like I love Missy. I'm a vet. I love animals. It's what I do. And you have one of the smartest, most beautiful dogs I've ever met." Then I stopped still, the fight was gone from my voice. I sighed. "I know you loved Rosie, and I don't doubt that she was special. But you're missing what's right in front of you. You're missing out on Brady, and Isaac, he's wonderful."

Isaac stood with his back to me. I couldn't see just how much my words affected him, but I had no doubt they'd found their mark. Good. I needed to say them, and he needed to hear them.

I called for Missy, who came to my side immediately. I guess I'd just drawn a line, and now it was up to him to decide. "Isaac, I'll call after work on Tuesday," I told him from the front door. "You can tell me then if you still want to be with me or not."

## 13

I got home, and instead of taking Missy for her usual walk, we jogged. Despite walking the entire day through the park, I needed to release this negative energy.

Isaac. Fucking hell. What an impossible man.

I knew he had his reasons, but for how long should I justify his bad behavior? His hurtful behavior?

I just didn't know.

Mark phoned that night, being a Sunday, like he always did. He could tell something was off. "What's up?"

I groaned. "Isaac."

"Oh," he said quietly. "What did he do now?"

Mark knew everything. He knew of our disagreements, he knew of Isaac's self-imposed distance with Brady, he knew of Isaac's tendency to overreact. He knew how much I loved him.

So I told him what had happened, of the beautiful day we'd had, how it all went pear-shaped when I'd shown some affection to Brady. I told him what I'd said and how I gave him 'til Tuesday to decide if he still wanted me.

"You know what you need?" Mark asked.

"I need to go there on Tuesday, be cool, calm, and collected and tell him no more games. I need to be strong and not give into him," I answered. "I need to tell him to pull his head out of his ass and he can start by loving his fucking dog." And then I added, more of an afterthought, "Then I'll tell him I love him."

Mark laughed. "Yes, that sounds all terribly mature, but I was thinking of something else you need."

I almost didn't want to know. "What's that?"

"Me!"

I smiled. Having Mark around sure sounded good, but with our jobs and the distance between us, it didn't seem likely. "Thanks for the offer."

"I'm being serious!" he cried into the phone. "I have to go in tomorrow, there's some staff management meeting going on which I'll need to be there for, but I can take the rest of the week off and come over."

"Really?"

"Yes really," he said. "We've been quiet at work, and the boss was only saying last week we should look at some vacation time soon."

I smiled. "That sounds great."

∾

I didn't have any missed calls or voice mails from Isaac on Monday, and I didn't try to call him either. I considered phoning Hannah on Monday night, just to see how he was, but stopped myself.

Work on Tuesday dragged until after lunch when Mark arrived. I told him to come around to the hospital so he could pick up a key to my house, because I'd be going to see Isaac and would be home late. He managed to meet Rani, Kate in reception, and Luke, the third year grad student. He also managed not to sexually harass any of them. He was courteous and pleasant, though he grinned at me like the devil himself.

I led him into my office for some privacy and so I could grab my keys. "Oh," he said, disappointed. "I thought you'd want me in an exam room so you could bend me over a table and take my temperature."

I grinned at him. "Tell me why I've missed you?"

He beamed. "Because I'm awesome!"

I laughed and unthreaded my front door key off my keychain, then handed it to him. "I would say 'make yourself at home' but I have no doubt you will."

He grinned. "Of course I will."

"There's wood inside for the fire, and you can take Missy for a walk if you want."

"But it's raining," he said. "And cold!"

"Missy won't mind."

He narrowed his eyes at me. "Will you bring home pizza?"

"Yes."

"And beer?"

I rolled my eyes. "There's beer in the fridge."

He grinned. "Deal." He pocketed the key and clapped one hand on my arm. "You'll be fine with Isaac, don't stress."

"Yeah, I know."

"Just stay strong, remember all that shit you were gonna tell him, and say everything you want to say before you shag him," he said seriously. "And most importantly, for God's sake, no olives on my pizza."

I rolled my eyes. "Thanks, man."

He opened my office door, ready to leave. "And Carter?"

"Yeah?"

"Tell him I said hi."

I smiled. "I will."

"Good," he said, walking down the hallway, away from me. "Now get back to work, they're not payin' ya to stand around talking all day."

I was still grinning when Rani came in to tell me my next appointment was waiting. She eyed me cautiously. "Was your visitor someone special?" she asked, trying to act nonchalant. "I mean he was cute and all, but not as cute as Isaac Brannigan."

I stared at her then shook my head. "Your fishing skills are lacking tact, Rani."

She grinned. "Just curious."

"No," I answered a smile. "My visitor, as you called him, was my best friend, Mark. He's staying with me for the week."

"And Isaac?" she asked, pretending not to be too interested.

"I'm seeing him this afternoon." I didn't bother telling her he might very well break up with me.

She grinned. "Oh, Isaac coming here, walking in the rain to see you, was the sweetest thing I've ever seen."

I rolled my eyes. Yes, it was sweet, he could be incredibly sweet. But he could also be incredibly insensitive and wounding. And that's what I was going to his place to sort out.

∼

As I arrived at Isaac's, I wondered how things would go, how he'd react, and what he'd decided. I had no idea if he'd tell me he didn't think we were working out, or if he'd apologize. Or both. That was the thing with Isaac, how he'd respond was anyone's guess.

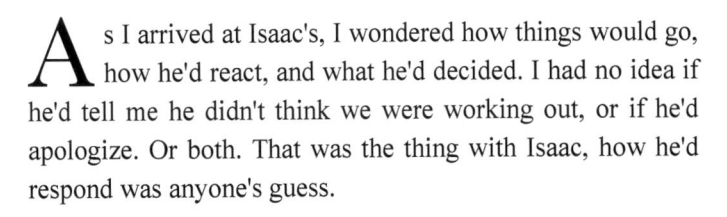

I hoped he'd say he wanted this to work, that he wanted *us* to work. I was looking forward to seeing him. I missed him. But the little bit of distance was also a good thing. It helped with perspective, and hopefully gave him time to think about what I'd said to him.

Hannah's car was still out front, and when she answered the door to let me in, I could tell things were tense between them.

"Thank God you're here," she said. "You might be able to talk some sense into him."

"Oh, for God's sake, Hannah," Isaac yelled back from the living room. "I told you not to say anything. I haven't decided, I told you that!"

I walked in, hesitating on who I should speak to. "Um, hello?"

"Just ignore her," Isaac told me. "We were just discussing something, and she doesn't agree with me, which is nothing unusual."

Hannah groaned in frustration. "Isaac, you just don't want to say anything in front of Carter because you know damn well he'll agree with me."

"Hannah, I said drop it," Isaac snapped at his sister. Then he turned toward me. "Carter, please come in and sit down. How was work?"

"Um, I can come back…"

Ignoring me completely, Isaac said, "No, Hannah was just leaving."

She snatched her bag off the counter. She was royally pissed off. I'd never seen her so mad. "You know what, Isaac? How about I don't come back this week? If you're so fucking independent and able, that you don't need me *or* Brady, then you can get yourself to work and home again, do all your own fucking housework, because I'm done." Hannah pointed to her brother, "I'll tell Carter, because I know damn well you won't, but Isaac here, in all his infinite fucking wisdom, wants to give Brady back."

I blinked, trying to get my head around what Hannah just said. I looked at Isaac. "You what?"

"Yep, you heard correctly," she said, answering for him. "Of all the stupid, spiteful, fucking *idiotic* things I've heard." She stomped over to the front door. "You think you can manage without Brady and me, Isaac? Well, good luck at the grocery store," she yelled, and she slammed the door behind her.

Isaac tried to look composed, but I could see he was hurt. He was quiet for a long moment then he said, "Sorry about that."

"Isaac, are you okay?"

"I'm fine," he answered quickly. "We have a blow out every couple of months. She'll yell, I'll yell, we'll both apologize and we're back to good again."

I nodded, not terribly convinced. "What did she mean? You want to give Brady back?"

His shoulders fell and he sighed. "I said I haven't decided anything."

I shook my head. "Why would you even consider it?"

Isaac frowned. "Can we not talk about this, please?"

He was obviously upset over the fight he'd just had with Hannah, but I couldn't let it go. "Isaac, I think we need to talk about it."

His jaw clenched. "Well, I don't want to talk about it."

I took a deep breath, remembering to keep my cool so we could discuss our problems calmly. "Isaac, if we're boyfriends, or partners, then we need to discuss these things," I said softly. Then I thought, maybe I should start at the beginning. "Is that what we are, Isaac?" I asked. "Did you still want to be with me?"

"Yes," he said with a nod. He reached out his hand, looking for mine, so I threaded my fingers with his. He smiled. "Yes, that's what I want."

"It's what I want too, Isaac," I told him. "I want to be with you."

He squeezed my hand. "It doesn't mean we'll always agree on things."

"I don't expect us to agree on everything," I replied. "In fact, I like debating things with you. But it does mean we need to be open and honest with each other."

He was quiet again, then he sighed. "I'm sorry about Sunday. We were having such a good weekend, and I ruined it. I'm sorry."

"Isaac," I said softly. "That's part of the problem. You'll fly off the handle, lose your temper, say something horrible, then apologize and just expect it to be okay again."

He nodded, but said nothing.

"You know, last weekend was wonderful," I told him, playing with his fingers. "You topped me," I said quietly. "And it was amazing, then we spent the day hiking in the park and it was so perfect. I thought 'oh, my god, I could see myself spending forever with you' and then one comment about Brady, and you're back to giving me the silent treatment."

I squeezed his hand. "It's a constant push and pull with you, Isaac. And quite frankly, it's draining."

His eyebrows furrowed. "You're not perfect either, you know."

I smiled. "I know I'm not."

"You snore."

I huffed in defeat. "Do I?"

He nodded. "Yep."

I shook my head at his attempt to sway me. "I don't expect you to be perfect, Isaac."

He snorted, sarcastically. "Well, you lucked out on that, you know, because I'm blind."

"Hey, that's not fair," I said, squeezing his hand again. "I've never cared about that, and you know it."

He nodded and sighed. "Yeah, I know. You've always been great about my blindness."

"It's just part of who you are," I told him. "It doesn't define you."

"Carter, it's not just the blindness I struggle with," he murmured. Isaac was quiet, then he frowned. "I spent a lot of years in therapy, dealing with… *stuff* from the accident. The death of my mother, and then my father. I know I have issues with… attachment. Maybe I should go back to see my therapist. I'm sure Hannah wouldn't disagree."

"Isaac, you don't need therapy, you just need to talk to me," I said, taking his hand in both of mine. "And Hannah. You just need to talk about what's bothering you and not bottle it up inside. Because when you do finally say something, it all comes out misdirected."

He nodded and whispered, "I know. I don't mean to."

"I know, baby." I leaned in and kissed the side of his head. "Please just talk to me." And then, while the iron was hot, I went back to Brady. "Isaac, what did you mean about giving Brady back?"

He took his hand from mine and put it in his lap. "I haven't decided anything yet," he started quietly. "But maybe it'd be best if I told the Guide Dogs Association we're not compatible…"

My heart sank. "Isaac, no…"

He shrugged. "You're right. I'm not being fair to him."

I sat side on so I faced him and took both his hands. "You're not being fair to yourself, either," I told him. "Please don't make any rash decisions because you're upset with me or Hannah."

"It's not that," he replied. "I don't think I was ready for another dog."

"Yes, you were," I said adamantly. "Isaac, I know you love him. I know you do. You just need to let yourself. You're a wonderful team. I've seen you out there on the hiking trails. I've seen you two work together. You're a perfect match."

He shrugged indifferently, but said nothing.

"And this is what you and Hannah fought about?"

"Yeah," he admitted. Then he shrugged again. "At the end of the day, it's not your decision, or Hannah's. It's mine."

"You'd be making the wrong decision," I told him. "Brady loves you."

He lifted his chin defiantly. "Like I said, I haven't decided."

"If you can let yourself love me, why can't you love him?" I asked.

Isaac wouldn't answer.

I shook my head. Here we were, back to Isaac the Impossible. Not sure I'd resolved anything, I sighed. "Isaac, I have to go. Mark's visiting. It was an impromptu visit; he got here this morning. I told him I wouldn't be here long."

"Oh," he mumbled.

I was hesitant to leave him. "Will you be okay?"

"Carter, I'm fine," he said.

God forbid I treat him like he's anything short of capable. I ran my hands through his hair. "Are you sure you and Hannah will be okay?" I asked. "How will you get to work tomorrow?"

"I'll call her later, give her some time to calm down," he said quietly. "If not, I can always catch the bus."

I shook my head, grateful for once he couldn't see just how frustrated, infuriated and disappointed I was. "Isaac, please tell me you'll call me if you need anything."

He nodded. "I'll be fine."

"Isaac—"

"I don't need a babysitter!" he snapped at me.

I sighed. "See? That right there, where you bite my head off, has to stop."

"Then don't treat me like a child."

"Then don't act like one." I stood up, putting some distance between us. "Isaac, you're not a child, and you don't need babysitting. But being blind means there are concessions for health and safety, not because you're incompetent. There's a difference. I'm concerned because I care."

I knelt down in front of him and took his hands. "Isaac, I love you, but I won't stand for the temper tantrums anymore. Okay? I love you, Isaac, that hasn't changed. But I'm going home now, and I think it might be a good idea if I don't come around until the weekend. But I want to talk to you every night on the phone, okay?"

He frowned, upset. "Why?"

"Because I want us to learn to talk to each other, to discuss things, to have proper communication, and talking over the phone is a good way to start. Plus, I want to hear your voice, and because I miss you when we don't talk every day."

He gave me a small smile. "Okay."

I leaned in and kissed him softly. "Now with Brady, maybe if Hannah doesn't drive you to work, taking the bus to work will give you a good opportunity to test just how good you two are together. Can you try that for me?"

He was quiet, but then nodded. His voice was quiet. "Maybe."

I smiled. *Maybe.* It wasn't a definitive yes, but with Isaac, *maybe* was a start. I kissed him sweetly.

"I should go," I told him. "But please promise you'll call me if you need anything."

∼

"How'd things go with Isaac?" Mark asked from the couch. He was lying down like he owned it, petting Missy, who was sprawled out in front of him.

I put the pizza down on the coffee table and fell into the other sofa with a sigh. "Okay. We determined that he can be difficult, that I snore, that we really need to talk more, and that we'd like to try and make it work."

"That's good, isn't it?" he asked. "So what's wrong?"

He knew me well. "He's considering taking Brady back, claiming incompatibility."

Mark sat up and stared at me. "He *what?*"

My head fell back on the sofa, and I sighed. "He just needs to realize what a good dog Brady is. How perfect they are together."

Mark frowned. "What will it take, do you think, for him to realize that?"

I shrugged. "I don't know."

Unfortunately, two days later, we found out.

## 14

The next day at work was normal. I saw and treated a variety of dogs, cats, ferrets, birds, and hamsters. Mark spent the day in the city then picked up some take-out for dinner, and we laughed and talked bullshit while we ate.

I tried calling Isaac before we walked Missy, but there was no answer, so I tried again after. It rang out every time.

I frowned at the phone. Mark, who was mumbling about having to walk a dog in the fucking Boston winter, stopped his bitching about the weather and asked, "What is he giving you the silent treatment for now?"

I pulled off my coat and sighed. "I don't know."

Mark shook his head. "I thought you said the childish games were over."

"That's what I thought." Then I added, "I wonder if he's okay. He was taking the bus, I think. Maybe I should call Hannah."

Mark raised an eyebrow. "And I thought you were supposed to not be babysitting him."

I sighed again. "I know."

"Try him again later," Mark reasoned. "Maybe he's in the shower, or on the crapper or something."

"Yeah, maybe," I conceded, not even acknowledging his crass phrasing.

He clapped a hand on my shoulder. "Go take a shower and try calling him again later." He shook his head with a knowing smile. "If you baby him one day after he tells you not to, he'll hand you your ass. And not in a good way."

I chuckled, despite myself. And after getting his voice-mail one more time, and even though it was late, I sent Hannah a text. *Have you heard from Isaac today?*

I fell asleep, waiting for a reply.

~

I checked my phone again before I walked into work. Still no reply from Isaac, and no reply from Hannah. I was starting to wonder if it was a Brannigan family trait.

I threw my keys, wallet, and phone in my desk drawer, and set about my usual day. It was maybe an hour later, just as I'd walked into the waiting room to collect my next patient, that Kate in reception called out to me.

"Dr Reece?" she said. "Phone call. It's Hannah Brannigan. She says it's important."

I picked up the receiver. "Hannah?"

"Yes, oh thank God, Carter, I've been trying your cell. I only saw your message an hour ago," she said in a rush. Her tone of panic sent a cold shiver through me. "It's Isaac."

"What about him?"

"I don't know where he is."

"You what?"

She started to cry. "His work called me this morning, asking if he was okay. He called in sick yesterday. He never went to work. He *never* doesn't go to work, Carter. Then he didn't go in again today, but he didn't call. So they called me to see how he was." She took a sobbing breath. "I'm at his house. He's not here, and Brady's not here either."

I could feel my heart get tight and thump hollow in my chest. "Hannah, you need to call the police. If he got on a bus, they have footage. You need to tell them—"

Then the phone started to beep. Hannah gasped, "I've got an incoming call. Maybe it's him. I'll call you right back." And the phone went dead in my ear.

I looked to Kate, who was staring at me, having just heard my half of the conversation. "Pass me the phone," I said. "I'll need to leave," I told Kate, as I took the phone and pressed numbers into it. "Cancel my appointments." Then Mark answered his phone. "Mark, it's me. Listen, Isaac's missing—"

And no sooner had the words come out of my mouth, than a policeman came through the door, with a dog covered in mud, dirt, and leaves, wearing a guiding harness. There was no mistaking him.

Brady.

"Mark, I have to go," I whispered and handed the phone back to Kate.

Then Rani was beside me. "Okay, bring him in through here," she directed the officer through to my exam room.

"You know this dog?" the policeman asked.

"Of course we know this dog," Rani told him.

"The owner of this guy said you'd know him here," the officer said.

I could finally make myself speak. "The owner, the man with this dog, where is he?" I asked. "Is he okay?"

"The blind guy?" The policeman asked, putting Brady down on the exam table. "He's okay, I think. They were taking him to Carney Hospital. Fell down an embankment at Wompatuck State Park, spent the night there. Paramedics said this guy here," he gave Brady a pat on the forehead, "kept him warm all night. Probably saved his life."

I sucked back a shaky breath, and Brady barked.

In the six months I'd known Brady, it was the first time I'd ever heard him bark. He stood there, all covered in dirt and muck, wagging his tail as though he was pleased to see me, and he barked again. It was like he was trying to tell me what he'd done, or that Isaac was hurt.

"I know, buddy," I told him, giving him a hug and a pat.

I turned to look at the others in the room. "Rani, I need my phone, please," I asked. "It's in my desk drawer." She was gone through the door, and I started to check Brady over. His mouth was clear, his tongue and gums were a healthy pink, his nose was wet. His eyes and ears were fine. He seemed okay, no contusions, no obvious injuries. But I wanted to be sure.

Rani was back with my phone, and I pressed Hannah's number. It went straight through to voicemail. "Hannah, Isaac's at Carney Hospital. Brady's with me. Call me."

"You know this dog?" the officer asked me again. "As in, you know the owner well enough to have contact numbers in your cell?"

I nodded, still looking over Brady. "Isaac Brannigan, the blind guy, as you put it, is my boyfriend."

Rani snapped her fingers at Kate, who stood dumbfounded in the doorway. "Prep x-ray. We'll need full scans."

"Oh." The policeman blinked in surprise.

I stared at him. "Is he injured? Was he pushed, or did he fall? Did he say what happened?"

The officer shook his head. "Said he fell. There are all these signs saying the trails were closed due to the recent

*Blind Faith*

rain, but signs are no good to a blind man." He shrugged one shoulder. "Some hikers found him this morning. Nothing broken, damn near frozen to death, but other than that, he said he was okay. More worried about his dog than himself."

My eyes burned, but I refused to cry. I had to hold myself together.

The policeman continued, "Mr Brannigan told us specifically to bring him here, said you'd know what to do. Sorry, I can't tell you much more." He smiled, "But if you're right with the dog, I'll be going."

Taking a deep breath, I looked at the police officer. "Thank you."

Rani put her hand on my arm. "We'll get him x-rayed, make sure everything's where it should be, then we can feed him. If he spent all day and night out, he'll be hungry. Then we can get him all cleaned up."

I nodded. "Thanks, Rani."

My assistant smiled at me. "It's fine. I can look after Brady, if you want to go."

I nodded. "I'll check his x-rays, then I'll go," I told her. "If you could get him cleaned up, make sure he's warm, hydrated. I'll come back and get him later, he can come home with me."

I was looking at Brady's x-rays when Kate bought Mark into my exam room. He didn't give her time to explain. "What the bloody hell, Carter?"

I spun around to look at him, and he didn't give me a chance to explain either.

"You call me, tell me Isaac's missing and then just hang up? I came down here at light speed," he cried. Then he noticed the dog on the exam table being inspected by Rani, and looked at me with wide eyes. "Is that Brady?" He went straight to him, giving the muddy dog a pat.

I nodded. "I was just checking his x-rays. They're all clear."

Mark looked from Brady to me. "Where the fuck is Isaac?"

"Carney Hospital."

"And what the fucking hell are you still doing here?"

"I'm heading in right now, but I had to check Brady. If I went in there and told him I didn't know how he was or that I'd just left him, he'd be so pissed at me," I told him. "Anyway, it's been no more than ten minutes. I'd only be sitting in a waiting room." As soon as I said it, I knew how ridiculous it sounded.

"Come on, I'll drive," Mark said, shaking his head. "You know, I've said this before, but for someone as smart as you, you're pretty fucking stupid."

Rani smiled then patting my arm, she told me, "He looks fine, just dirty, had a rough night. I'll get him fed and cleaned and beautiful, ready for you to pick him up."

I gave her a watery smile. "Thank you." Then I patted Brady, rested my forehead on his, and told him, "I'll tell him you're okay."

Mark grabbed my arm, pulling me away. "Very touching, Dr Doolittle, but get your ass in the car."

∼

I've always hated hospitals. I mean, no one *loves* hospitals. I called Hannah from the car and this time she answered. She was already there, telling me they were just taking him from emergency up to a room, so we knew where to go when we got there.

The smell and the too-damn-slow elevators alone were enough to make anyone hate hospitals. But when I rounded the corner and almost ran into room eleven, I'd never been so happy to be in a hospital in my life.

Hannah stood up to greet me. She'd been crying, her eyes were red and puffy, and when she saw me, she started to cry again. I was quick to put my arms around her, but I couldn't take my eyes off the man on the bed. He was lying on his side, facing us.

"Isaac," I said his name softly.

He smiled a little, though he looked tired and beat. "Hey."

I let go of Hannah and touched the side of Isaac's face. "You scared me."

His brow furrowed, he frowned and nodded. "Sorry."

"Hey, don't be sorry," I told him softly. "I'm just glad you're okay. Are you hurt anywhere?"

He shook his head and took my hand from his face, to hold in his. His voice was quiet. "No, I just ache all over. The doctor said it's from being cold for too long. They're keeping me in overnight, just to monitor the circulation in my hands and feet." Then he asked, "Is Mark here? I thought I heard two people walk in."

I looked at my friend, who still stood in the doorway, and smiled at him. Mark came in and stood beside me. If he was shocked to see Isaac's stark blue eyes, he never let on.

"Yeah, I'm here. Someone had to drive this useless lump in, or he'd still be walking around in circles at the animal hospital."

That reminded me. "Isaac, I've seen Brady," I told him.

His eyes opened, worry was clear on his face. "Is he okay? I asked he get taken to you."

"He's fine," I reassured him. "Baby, he's just fine. I did a full x-ray and left him with Rani to get cleaned up. I'll pick him up tonight and take him back to my place."

Isaac nodded, took the hand of mine he held, and put it on his face. He closed his eyes. "Thank you."

Seeing him just lying there, without his sunglasses, with his blindness exposed, he seemed so vulnerable. He hated people seeing him without his glasses; he felt more protected when he wore them. I wanted to protect him. I needed to be closer, to feel him against me, to know he was safe and, by the way he held my hand, I'd say he needed it too.

I climbed up onto the bed, slid my arm underneath his head and wrapped my other arm around his waist.

"How about we go grab a coffee?" Mark said to Hannah. He put his arm around her and led her to the door.

"Mark, she's married, remember?" I called out after them.

"That's okay," he answered. Then I heard him ask, "Is your husband cute?"

I chuckled at Mark, and even Isaac smiled. I rubbed his back and kissed the top of his head. "Did you want to talk about what happened?"

He was quiet for a moment, then he took a deep breath, and told me. Everything.

"I kept thinking about what you said," he started. "That I should use this time Hannah wasn't there, to see if Brady and I were truly compatible. So I thought of Wompatuck." He sighed. "We'd been there just recently, so I knew Brady was familiar with it, and you made us take the bus before, which I presumed was for Brady's benefit as well as mine."

I smiled and tightened my hold on him.

"Anyway," he continued softly. "We got there around ten-ish. We took the paved path first and that was fine. But then I decided to see if Brady was really as good as you said he was, so we went to the far trail." He took a deep breath. "Apparently there were signs saying the trail was closed. There'd been track slippage."

I spoke then. "I can't believe they didn't have gates or barricades, something other than just a sign. It's not good enough, and really, someone should be held accountable."

"Yeah," Isaac agreed quietly. "Me."

"What?"

"I was so stupid," he admitted. "I knew better, but I was trying to prove a point. It was dangerous and stupid." He shook his head, burrowing himself into me. "I knew I had to be back at the bus stop by three, before it got too cold, so I was probably going faster than I should have. We got about halfway, and I could feel the ground starting to compromise. Brady kept trying to stop me…"

Then he started to cry. "He kept stopping, but I kept pushing him, telling him yes. I made him go. We got to the point where he wouldn't move, and I got mad at him. I yelled at him to go forward, but he stayed put. I pulled on the harness and over-stepped," he said, as his tears soaked my shirt. "I slid down the side of the trail. It must have been forty feet down. It was mostly mud, and it was cold. I lost my phone."

"Oh, baby," I said, trying not to cry myself.

"I listened for a passerby, I listened for anyone, but there was nothing. Then Brady was beside me. He came down for me. He tried to help me up, but it was slippery and too steep. I didn't know if there was a further drop off, so I didn't want to move. I was so scared," he sobbed, clutching on to me. "Carter, I was so scared."

I couldn't stop my tears. I couldn't even imagine what he'd been through. It would have been terrifying being able to see, let alone going through it blind. I just held him tighter.

Isaac shook his head and continued to cry while he talked. "Brady wouldn't leave me. He stayed with me. He almost laid on top of me, keeping me warm. It was so fucking cold, but he stayed with me." He sniffled and took a shaky breath. "You were right, and Hannah. You both were. He's a good dog, he's such a good dog, and I've been so horrible to him all this time."

I kissed the top of his head and rubbed my hand over his back. "Brady knows you love him."

Isaac shook his head and cried harder. "I can't believe I even considered getting rid of him, just because we kept fighting over him. I thought if he was out of the equation, we wouldn't fight. God, how deluded was that?" He sucked back a shaky sob. "I can't believe I was so horrible to him, and he stayed with me, down that muddy embankment, he kept me warm. God, Carter, what a mess I made of everything."

"Shh, baby," I whispered soothingly, rubbing my hand over his back and through his hair. "Everything's fine now. You're safe, Brady's safe." I kissed his forehead again. "Go to sleep, baby."

I pulled up the blanket, and Isaac snuggled into the crook of my arm, sniffling and sobbing quietly. Soon his breathing evened out, and he'd all but cried himself to sleep. I didn't want to move, I didn't want to risk waking him. I wanted him to lie in my arms, where he felt safe and loved, forever.

~

"I can't believe you're doing this," I mumbled, shaking my head.

"It'll save time and paperwork," Mark replied. He looked around the hospital parking lot, put his sunglasses on, and took Brady's harness.

The dog shook himself, as though he knew this was a bad joke, but like me, was unable to stop him.

"Come on," Mark said. "You want to see your boy, don't you?"

"Well, yes," I answered. "Of course I do."

"Then quit your bitching," he quipped. "And walk with a blind man."

I rolled my eyes. "Being blind at a nightclub on weekends doesn't count."

Mark laughed, but still walked into the hospital, pretending to be blind. And we were officially going to hell.

I wanted to bring Brady in for Isaac, and Mark thought... well, actually Mark rarely thought anything through.

We walked through the front doors of the hospital and headed down a corridor. Mark nodded to two female nurses, smiled back at one little old lady, and walked right up to the elevator doors, reached out and pressed the button. "For God's sake, Mark," I hissed at him. "If you're going to pretend to be blind, stop acting like you can see."

"Oh."

"And you think I'm stupid."

The elevator doors opened, and we stepped inside and Mark laughed. "You know, instead of taking Missy to pick up chicks or dicks, I should take Brady, throw on some sunglasses. My God, imagine all the good Samaritan's I could pick up."

I sighed. "You are going to hell."

He laughed again, and as the elevator doors opened, we walked toward Isaac's room.

He was sitting up in bed, dressed in normal clothes, looking much brighter. "Hey," I said, and I walked over and gave him a kiss. "Good morning. We brought someone in to see you."

Isaac smiled. "I thought I heard nails clicking on the linoleum floor."

So, breaking nearly every health code the hospital had, I lifted Brady up and put him on the bed. Unsure of being up so high or on a bed, Brady lowered to his belly and crawled up to Isaac, who threw his arms around him. He hugged him and Brady's tail thumped madly, both equally happy to see the other.

"Oh, Brady," Isaac said. "You're such a good boy."

I'm not sure who was smiling the biggest, Isaac or Brady. Or me.

"Hannah's putting on a big welcome home lunch," I told him. "We better bust you out, huh?"

Isaac grinned and gave Brady another hug. He ruffled the fur on the dog's forehead. "You ready to go home, boy?"

Brady licked his face, making Isaac pull back in shock. I laughed. "I think that's a yes."

## SIX WEEKS LATER

We heard a car pull up in front of Isaac's house, and he smiled. The sound was familiar to Isaac, even with tires crunching on snow. "That's Max."

I got up and looked through the window. It certainly was.

After his overnight adventure at the hiking trail, Isaac had phoned Dr Fields for the first time since his retirement. They'd spoken a few times over the phone since, and this was the second time the older man had come to visit.

The first visit he'd made was not long after the accident. Isaac had been told to stay at home and rest the week after getting out of hospital. He'd thought it was unnecessary of course, even argued with the doctor, but eventually relented. He had spent the time resting, reading, and planning classes. But he'd also used the time to do some fun things with Hannah; they'd gone for coffee, to the movies, cooked up a freezer full of food. It had been good to see them get back to being brother and sister, friends even, without being the blind man and his caregiver.

But Dr Fields had also visited. Isaac had called and apologized for not calling sooner. He'd explained what happened at the state park, and Dr Fields had worriedly come to visit that same afternoon.

He had been shocked, Isaac told me afterward. "But nowhere near as shocked as he was when I told him we were dating."

I hadn't known whether to laugh or bang my head on the table. But what was done was done, and after a stunned silence, the old man had taken the news well, apparently. As well as he could, all things considered.

Isaac had simply told him, in the matter-of-fact way he does, that I was quite possibly the best thing to ever happen to him. Isaac had told him he meant no offense, but Max retiring had turned out to be a blessing in disguise. Dr Fields had laughed, Isaac said. By the end of the afternoon, things between them were back to the way they always had been.

Isaac greeted Dr Fields at the door. "Come on in."

The older man walked in with a large square parcel in his hands. It looked kind of heavy. I quickly went to him and took the brown paper-wrapped box. "Here, let me take that for you."

He smiled. "Thanks, Carter. It's a box of concrete, or as we call it in our house, my wife's fruit cake."

I chuckled but put the heavy box on the kitchen counter. It felt like concrete.

"Helen insisted I bring some," the older man went on to say. "Hope you don't mind."

"Not at all," Isaac answered. "Thank you." He sat down on the sofa. "So Max, how did you spend the holidays?"

Dr Fields sat back on the sofa with a groan. "Well, the grandkids came, made noise, made a mess, more noise," he said with a smile. "But it was lovely. How about you? How was your Christmas?"

"It was great," Isaac told him. "We got some exciting

news. Hannah and Carlos are expecting their first child in July. I'm going to be an uncle."

Dr Fields grinned. "Oh, that's marvelous! Tell her I said congratulations!"

"I will," Isaac reassured him. "Apart from that, we just spent it here; me and Carter, Hannah and Carlos. Family lunch, then dinner. It was really nice."

And it had been. It'd been quiet, we'd exchanged small gifts, ate too much food, spoiled the dogs rotten, and ate some more.

Dr Fields then turned his attention to me. "How've you been, Carter? How's the shop going?"

I smiled. "I've been really well, thanks. And work's been really busy, as I'm sure you know, but it's running smoothly. You really should come in sometime. I'm sure the staff would love to see you."

"Oh, I don't want to impose," he said with a smile.

"You're certainly not imposing," I told him. "Mrs Yeo asks about you."

"Oh, the little old dear," he said fondly. "How's she doing? How's Mr Whiskers?"

"Mr Whiskers passed away," Isaac said gently. "That'd be about three months ago now."

"Oh, no," Dr Fields frowned.

"Sorry I didn't call you," I offered. "I meant to let you know."

"That's okay," the old man said. "It must have been sad for her."

"Yeah, it was sad," I agreed. "But I kept calling in to see her every second Thursday. You know she has no close family, and she's ninety-two. And then just before Christmas, Isaac thought it might be a nice idea if we got her another companion. So three weeks ago, we got her one."

Dr Fields looked at Isaac, clearly surprised, and a slow smile spread across his face. "Really? Another cat?"

I nodded. "Yes, we found a five-year-old rescued tabby that apparently didn't get on with kids, and we figured, considering Mrs Yeo didn't get on with children either, they'd be a good match."

Dr Fields smiled. "And how'd they go?"

"Well," I told him. "She cried, of course, but when we left, Tiddles was asleep on the chair in front of the fire and Mrs Yeo was already making plans to cook more fish at Christmas."

Dr Fields looked at me then Isaac, and he smiled. "So, it's New Year's Eve," he said. "Got any wild and crazy plans?"

Isaac scoffed. "Hardly. Carter's taking me somewhere, won't tell me where exactly."

I grinned. "How about I brew some coffee?" I stood up and walked into the kitchen, successfully avoiding that subject.

Isaac groaned in frustration. He'd been pestering me all day about where I was taking him, but they soon started chatting while I puttered in the kitchen. I fought with the coffee machine, took the dogs outside for a pee, and when I came back inside, both dogs went into the living room where Isaac and Dr Fields were sitting.

Both men greeted both dogs, and I could see Dr Fields looking at Isaac, watching in wonder how he patted and spoke to Brady. He turned to look at me, with both eyebrows raised and smiling, and I gave him a nod.

"Sugar, cream?" I asked.

"Neither," the older man answered. "Black is fine."

"Would you like me to cut some of the fruit cake?" I asked Dr Fields.

"Good Lord, no," he replied, rubbing his stomach. "Use it as a doorstop or something."

I laughed and brought down three cups of steaming coffee, just as Isaac's phone rang in his pocket. The synthetic voice declared the caller to be Marianna, his boss.

"Excuse me," Isaac said. "I'll just take this in another room."

We watched him leave, and I could hear the beginning of the phone conversation. She must have been phoning to wish him a happy New Year, because Isaac quickly returned the sentiment.

Dr Fields cleared his throat, making me look at him. "Well, Carter," he started. "I have to say, I was shocked when he told me you were... *romantically* involved." He sipped his coffee, and I wondered for a brief moment how this conversation would go. But then he said, "What you do in your private life is no one else's business, but I'll tell you this," he looked toward the door Isaac just walked through, "the difference in that man from six months ago to now, is like night and day. I've known him for a lot of years, and I haven't seen him that happy in a long time." He smiled at me. "If ever."

I smiled back at him. "He's really coming along in leaps and bounds. He still has his snarky, snide moments, but he's learning to deal with his resentment and anger."

"Thanks to you," Dr Fields said.

I shook my head. "No, thanks to Brady," I told him. "You should see how they are together now."

The old man smiled just as Isaac walked back in.

"Sorry to keep you," he said, sitting back down. "Carter, Marianna said to say Happy New Year."

I smiled and handed him his coffee. We chatted a little bit longer while the dogs slept on the rug and when Dr Fields said goodbye, he promised to come in to the animal hospital to say hello.

Isaac had walked Dr Fields to the door while I took the empty cups to the sink. When he came back, he walked over, reached out for me, and slipped his arms around me, nuzzling into my neck.

"God, I love how you smell."

I chuckled. "Are you trying to butter me up so I'll tell you where I'm taking you?"

I could feel him smile against my neck. "No."

"Liar."

He chuckled. "Please?"

I sighed. "Okay," I relented. "We're going ice-skating."

He stood straight up, and his mouth fell open. "No, I'm not."

"Yes, you are."

"Mm mm," he shook his head. "Carter, I can't do that."

"Yes, you can," I said, tightening my arms around his waist. "We'll go ice-skating, and it will be fun and romantic, then we can come back here, get warm, have dinner, dance, make love until midnight." Then I whispered in his ear, "I want you inside me when the clock strikes twelve."

He shivered from head to foot and groaned. He was quiet for a moment before he asked, "What if I fall?"

I pulled him against me. "I'll never let you fall. I'll have hold of you."

"You won't let me go?"

I shook my head, and whispered. "Never."

## The End

## THE BLIND FAITH SERIES

∽

Book One - Blind Faith
Book Two - Through These Eyes
Book Three - Blindside: Mark's Story
Christmas Bonus - Twelfth of Never (free read)

∽

## ABOUT THE AUTHOR

N.R. Walker is an Australian author, who loves her genre of gay romance.
She loves writing and spends far too much time doing it, but wouldn't have it any other way.

She is many things: a mother, a wife, a sister, a writer. She has pretty, pretty boys who live in her head, who don't let her sleep at night unless she gives them life with words.

She likes it when they do dirty, dirty things... but likes it even more when they fall in love.

She used to think having people in her head talking to her was weird, until one day she happened across other writers who told her it was normal.

She's been writing ever since...

∽

*Contact the author*
nrwalker@nrwalker.net

## ALSO BY N.R. WALKER

*Blind Faith*
*Through These Eyes (Blind Faith #2)*
*Blindside: Mark's Story (Blind Faith #3)*
*Ten in the Bin*
*Point of No Return – Turning Point #1*
*Breaking Point – Turning Point #2*
*Starting Point – Turning Point #3*
*Element of Retrofit – Thomas Elkin Series #1*
*Clarity of Lines – Thomas Elkin Series #2*
*Sense of Place – Thomas Elkin Series #3*
*Taxes and TARDIS*
*Three's Company*
*Red Dirt Heart*
*Red Dirt Heart 2*
*Red Dirt Heart 3*
*Red Dirt Heart 4*
*Red Dirt Christmas*
*Cronin's Key*
*Cronin's Key II*
*Cronin's Key III*
*Exchange of Hearts*
*The Spencer Cohen Series, Book One*
*The Spencer Cohen Series, Book Two*

*The Spencer Cohen Series, Book Three*

*The Spencer Cohen Series, Yanni's Story*

*Blood & Milk*

*The Weight Of It All*

*Perfect Catch*

*Switched*

*Imago*

*Imagines*

*Red Dirt Heart Imago*

**Free Reads:**

*Sixty Five Hours*

*Learning to Feel*

*His Grandfather's Watch (And The Story of Billy and Hale)*

*The Twelfth of Never (Blind Faith 3.5)*

*Twelve Days of Christmas (Sixty Five Hours Christmas)*

**Translated Titles:**

*Fiducia Cieca (Italian translation of Blind Faith)*

*Attraverso Questi Occhi (Italian translation of Through These Eyes)*

*Preso alla Sprovvista (Italian translation of Blindside)*

*Il giorno del Mai (Italian translation of Blind Faith 3.5)*

*Cuore di Terra Rossa (Italian translation of Red Dirt Heart)*

*Cuore di Terra Rossa 2 (Italian translation of Red Dirt Heart 2)*

*Cuore di Terra Rossa 3 (Italian translation of Red Dirt Heart 3)*

*Confiance Aveugle (French translation of Blind Faith)*

*A travers ces yeux: Confiance Aveugle 2 (French translation of Through These Eyes)*

*Aveugle: Confiance Aveugle 3 (French translation of Blindside)*

*À Jamais (French translation of Blind Faith 3.5)*

*Cronin's Key (French translation)*

*Cronin's Key II (French translation)*

*Cronin's Key III (French translation)*

*Au Coeur de Sutton Station (French translation of Red Dirt Heart)*

*Partir ou rester (French translation of Red Dirt Heart 2)*

*Faire Face (French translation of Red Dirt Heart 3)*

*Rote Erde (German translation of Red Dirt Heart)*

*Rote Erde 2 (German translation of Red Dirt Heart 2)*

Printed in Poland
by Amazon Fulfillment
Poland Sp. z o.o., Wrocław